I0758181

CHARLEY'S
CONFESSION

ELIZABETH CHAYSE-WILLIAMS

Copyright © 2024 by Elizabeth Chayse Williams

All Rights Reserved

No portion of this book may be reproduced in any form without written permission from the publisher or author, except as permitted by US copyright law. No part of this publication may be reproduced, distributed, or transmitted in any form or by any means, including photocopying, recording, or other electronic or mechanical methods, without the prior written permission of the publisher, except as permitted by US copyright law. For permission requests, contact the author.

The story, all names, characters, and incidents portrayed in this production are fictitious. No identification with actual persons (living or deceased), places, buildings, and products is intended or should be inferred.

First edition 2024

ebook ISBN: 979-8-89316-425-1
paperback ISBN: 979-8-89316-426-8

DEDICATION

To the hearts that find strength in confession and
the souls unafraid of new love and change.
This is for you; may you always have the courage to
embrace
change and accept yourself just as you are.

AUTHOR'S NOTE

Dear Reader,

Thank you for stepping back into Charley's world with me. Writing *Charley's Confession* has been an emotional journey—one that's layered with confessions, chaos, and a whole lot of heart. I'm thrilled to share this next chapter of her story with you.

If you're curious about how it all began, don't miss *Nick's Confession*—the exclusive prequel that dives into Charley and Nick's high school days. It's packed with sparks, heartbreak, and the choices that shaped everything.

To claim your copy by signing up to my newsletter https://dashboard.mailerlite.com/forms/1055596/138 831126629188944/share

And speaking of what's next—keep an eye out for the next stories in Mountmooke Bay. The journey continues, full of twists, love, and new beginnings. I'd love to hear what you think! Your feedback means so much, and connecting with readers is one of my favorite parts of this process. Feel free to reach out any time.

Thank you for reading—I can't wait to hear your thoughts!

With love,

Elizabeth xoxo

Scan me!

The Mountmooke Series

Charley's Confession

Book One – The beginning of Charley and Drew.

Charley's Revelation

Book Two – When the truth finally surfaces, will love be enough to hold them together?

Charley's Devotion

Book Three – A story of found family and daily choices.

Nick's Confession (The Prequel)

Book Four – Charley's teenage years and how she met Nick. Download this as a gift when you sign up for my newsletter.

Charley's Collection

Book Five – Five women. One book club. Endless confessions. And a collection of stories they never meant to share.

CONTENTS

1

GOOD MORNING

CHARLEY

Unfamiliar warmth wraps around me, pulling me from my dreams. *Who's in my bed?* For a moment, I'm not alone. I twist slightly, savoring the sensation, my heart aching at the thought of how long it's been. It feels so real, so comforting after all the emptiness of the past mornings. *But it can't be.* It's just another dream. With a sigh, I pull the blanket tighter around my shoulders, sinking into the illusion, wishing I didn't have to wake up alone again.

He's holding me close. I sense his powerful arms embracing me, from my rib cage to my curvy hips. The feeling of being confined is something I love. I snuggle into my pillow, feeling his arm muscles flex and pulling me tighter, his body against my bare cheeks.

Let it happen.

His ragged breath tickles my shoulder and makes me wiggle slightly with excitement. I let my imagination run down this path. "Good, you're awake," he says into my ear, sending shivers down my spine.

The dirty girl inside me wakes up as I stretch, letting my hand trail down my body. The oversized T-shirt I wore as a nightie has ridden up, baring my stomach. My hand slides lower, and I'm reminded why I prefer to sleep bare. It's all about freedom and comfort. *We need to let things breathe!* My inner dirty girl chimes in.

I shift again, the plush blanket cocooning my shoulders. My hips move instinctively as I imagine the soft fabric of his boxers brushing against me, a gentle tease as I press closer, lying on my side.

With one eye barely open, I am greeted by the gentle glow of the morning sun creeping through my bedroom window. It was well past midnight when I finally crawled into bed, my mind racing with worry, until Troy returned home. I will deal with those mom issues later. I brush aside his curfew violation and let my mind wander back to the enticing daydream of having a man beside me in bed. I've been alone for a while now. Most men I've met don't want to date a mom with a teenager, but it sure would be comforting to have someone by my side. Holding me. *He'll settle right in behind you; wouldn't that feel good?*

He rubs my leg. I can feel myself relax into him. *He is here to take my troubles away in all ways possible.*

I groan, stretch, and reposition myself, imagining how I might feel the length of him on the back of my thigh. I picture his hand rubbing my hip and leg, and I try to stay still enough to let him explore.

"Touch me, please," I whisper.

His left hand finds its way under my T-shirt to caress me. As he rubs my breast slowly, I can feel the calluses on his palms against my bare skin. I soak in the sensation and imagine how his hands would feel on the warmth between my pressed thighs. I turn my torso toward him as he pinches my nipple between his thumb and index finger.

I gasp at the sensation, and he pulls me closer. As he puts my nipple in his mouth, I feel the gentle, firm pressure from his lips and tongue. My body aches, and I can feel the tingling between my legs like there is a direct line connecting these two points. It feels so good like he has been doing this forever.

Keep going; I need this.

I feel the nibble followed by a suck and search my brain for a witty way to tell him how much I like that.

Trust him to figure it out.

His mouth crashes into mine, silencing my brain with his demanding kisses. I'm hungry and try to place the salty taste of him.

Mmm, he has his own special taste. I want more.

The feisty vixen in me is starving. As he gets on top, I can feel his length pressing against me.

I need this so badly.

He pulls away momentarily, hovering above me. "God, I've wanted you for a long time, Charley."

I smile and sweetly say, "Now that you have me under you, whatever will you do next?"

He leans down and pins me to the mattress. "I want to taste every inch."

I buck slightly, testing whether I can move under this mountain of a man. His lips find mine again, and he holds my wrists over my head with one hand. I feel like he could hurt me if he wanted to. Maybe punish me for being a bad girl with naughty thoughts.

A very naughty girl.

He slowly moves down my body, and I hear him inhale. I wonder if I smell as good to him as he does to me. I inhale and imagine wood smoke and the freshness that comes after a rain.

His mouth nips at my hip as his free hand pushes my thigh to open my legs. My body shudders as it comes undone from his touch. I feel like I'm an instrument that he's trying to learn to play as he continues to caress me with kisses, testing each spot to see if it's the right note.

"Keep playing, please," I beg.

I break free of his grasp as his mouth finds its way between my legs, and I want to cry out with the explosion of pleasure he sends through my body. The small circles of his tongue are perfect; the pressure is perfect. He is perfect. I hook a hand under my thigh to pull my legs wider for him.

Dirty girl.

I'm getting lost in the sensation and wondering if I can finish like this.

No. Take control.

I move my hips to meet his mouth, wanting to grind and feel the stubble on his face. It's not enough. I need more.

TAKE CONTROL!

I can't help myself. This needs to be on my terms. Instead of bucking him off and flipping him on his back, I realize he is too large for my frame. I surprise him by grabbing his length. "I need to know you are worth it first. On your back."

He obeys my command, a thrill whooshing through me.

He is at my entrance, and I steady myself to help guide him inside. One inch at a time, he slips inside, and I gasp as his thick girth fills me. I pull myself up a bit to settle back down, watching his face change. I see his inner battle between his need to regain control and his curiosity about what will happen next. I grab his hands and put them on my tits. "Hold these for me, please. I need to ride."

I bounce and squeeze myself around him, enjoying how he fills me up. My control is faltering. I'm close to the edge, but my legs burn with exertion.

My stamina needs to be tested as I imagine his hands moving to my hips to help guide me. I can feel myself climbing toward orgasm as he fills me up. I speed up. My thighs ache, knowing I can't go much longer. The deep ache builds inside me. *Yes, yes, Andrew, YES!* I move to pinch my nipples to help intensify the wave; I can't stop it now.

Take what you want!

I let it crash over me, letting it out. The sweet feeling of release. But part of me can't stay quiet. *Andrew?* I wonder. *Where did that come from?*

I take a minute to regain my composure as I pull the vibrator out from inside me. My creamy white cum covers it. I wipe my favorite toy on my T-shirt nightie and set it back on my nightstand, thinking I'll clean it up better later. "Thanks for the help."

You might have taken the edge off... for now.

Andrew... Oh, God. I haven't thought about him in so long. I wonder how he popped into my head—the last I heard, he was in Colorado. He left Utah so quickly after we graduated from high school. *I wonder how he's doing.*

I see his grandmother, Martha, often. She is one of my regular customers who comes to the bookstore each month, teasing me about how I should open my own store someday. Maybe someday, but for now, I'm happy to help Mrs. Mahone. She has owned the Harbour Street Booknook for three decades. I couldn't imagine competing with her. I was expecting Martha last week, but she's been in the hospital after a nasty fall. I hope she didn't break anything. I'll have to ask around. *Maybe that's why Andrew is on my mind.*

I remind myself that Andrew isn't my fantasy man. I need to focus on finding someone in this town, someone who is available. Thank goodness my toys are at the ready, but now it's time to get to church.

You need to confess some sins, woman!

2

SPECIAL DELIVERY

ANDREW

I hate this place. The scent of disinfectants tries to mask the lingering odor of urine and sweat. I'll take the earthy grit of my helmet any day over this uneasy sterility. Why can't they crack a window in here?

I make my way down the hall, Bible in hand, toward the nurses' station. At Mountmooke General, each floor is the same. Some creative design techs must have thought it was revolutionary when they built it in the 1970s. It makes me hope that new hospital designs have better airflow.

Why does the smell stick in the air like that? *So familiar.* It floods me with memories of when I was here five years ago for Mom. A shiver runs down my back and I pray the presence who ferries souls isn't waiting for Gran.

Please be okay.

A few feet from the nursing station, I see one woman behind the kind of glass with a little hole to talk through. What's its purpose? Such a strange way to protect the workers inside this glass cage that looks more like a fishbowl. Maybe we are supposed to sit and observe the activity like at an aquarium. Nurse Fish... I smile inwardly at the stupidity.

I stand near the hole thinking she will want me to talk through it to ask my questions when it's my turn. I hear a steady beeping as she frantically writes and holds the phone between her ear and shoulder. I can't hear what she is saying, but she seems rushed, trying to end the conversation quickly as I approach. Is she a nurse? How do you tell? Do I say, 'Hello, nurse'?

Don't be weird.

I feel bad interrupting her, so I move a little off to the side to wait. I look for the entrance to the fishbowl, wondering how they get inside. Is there only one door? That's a fire hazard.

The beeping burrows into my brain, and I'm surprised she can focus with all the extra distractions. Can't she hear it? Can't she turn it off?

My thoughts are interrupted as she knocks on the glass to get my attention. She comes closer to the little hole, holding her hand over the receiver. A pause in her conversation.

"Hi, Andrew. Are you here to see your grandma?"

"Yes, room 308?"

She nods. How does she know my name? Am I supposed to know her? Maybe we went to school together. That was so long ago, and I've been gone. How am I supposed to remember everyone? No one should know me anymore.

She's a cute little thing and looks far too young for me. Maybe Gran told her I was coming, and I am being paranoid.

"Thank you," I say, grateful she doesn't make me sign in or ask me for details I don't want to give. She nods and goes back to the phone call, but not before I notice her rolling her bottom lip between her teeth. Damn.

The brass name tag on her uniform reads.... Jennifer RN. How many Jennifers have I met in my life?

Walk away.

I open the door to room 308 and see Gran sitting in the bed by the window. Propped up with a pillow and her glasses on the tip of her nose, doing the crossword. She insists it will help her brain, as she has told me hundreds of times when I ask her how it is going. It's how we start every conversation when I call her. "How are your puzzles coming?" She never boasts about her successes, but I know she competes with her friend Jean. She called me once when she solved the puzzle before Jean. She was likely relieved her brain wasn't broken in some strange way that has terrified her ever since she turned seventy-five.

Gran doesn't notice when I enter the room, trying to be quiet in my work boots. I should have changed out of my work clothes, but when I got the call saying she needed her Bible, I dropped everything and came right away. As I pass the first bed, I notice a person curled up asleep. I try to see their face since they look so frail and small.

Lord, please don't let Gran get like that.

Gran sees me, "Drew! I'm so happy you came." I go towards her and kiss her cheek, relieved when I notice she still smells like honey and sweetness. I am thankful the hot sickness scent has not enveloped her like it did when I saw my mother in a bed like this.

"Of course, emergency bible delivery," I say as I place it on her lap and pull up a chair.

"Thank you, dear. Those young boys wouldn't get it for me." I sense a little whine in her voice, so not like the strong-minded woman she usually portrays. She must not be feeling one hundred percent.

"Gran, it's not the paramedic's job. They grabbed your purse, though?"

"Yes, how ridiculous is it for me to think I need a bigger purse that holds more stuff," she chuckles.

"Well, hopefully, this never happens again."

"It was just my silly knee acting up," she trails off, and I wonder if she will finish the thought and tell me what else is bothering her. She is so closed-lipped about telling me about her medical issues. Like it's a big secret she can't share with me because I might not understand or because she is too proud to admit her faults.

"What did the doctor say?" I prompt, hoping she will let me in a little this time.

"Your Aunt Christine is coming in tomorrow for the scans. The doctor will talk to us afterwards," she trails off again.

"Scans?"

"I don't want to worry you dear; your aunt will be here. I'm sure all will be okay." She reaches for my hand and pats it a few times in a way I'm sure she thinks is reassuring; it feels a little dismissive.

"You know I can be here if you need me to." I hesitate, unsure if I want to be part of doctor's meetings again. There were so many after my parents' accident. My head swims with the thought.

"No, no. I need you to help get my house ready for me to come home. Can you do that for me, Andrew dear?"

She uses my given name. Now I'm more suspicious. I don't want to press the issue. I have a feeling she knows the post-accident memories are still a wound I carry.

Getting a phone call to tell me my parents were run off the road was something I'll never forget. My dad was killed instantly; my mother's brain injury killed her after six weeks of hospital hell.

"Yes, Gran, I'll do whatever I can to get you back home," I promise more to myself than to her.

"See, this is why you are my favorite. I'm happy you aren't rushing off to Denver so fast. Your brother can't seem to get here to help." A slight at her other grandson, who seems to disappear at the whisper of the word *hospitalized*. He has sent a few texts and offered to come... later. I can't blame him, but I also know that if my brother was here, *he* would be the favorite.

"I'm staying. There is no rush for me to head out; they gave me a leave of absence." I try to reassure her, knowing my captain will let me extend if I need to.

She sighs, letting her shoulders relax a little more into the pillows. "Did you see Jennifer at the desk? I told her my handsome grandson was coming in. She is such a sweet thing. Maybe you can take her on a date?"

I bristle, trying to compose myself before I remind her I just left my fiancé. There is NO WAY I'm interested in going on a 'date'. "Now I know you are feeling better if you are playing matchmaker."

"You need a nice girl, Andrew."

"How do you know she's a nice girl?" I ask, half expecting to hear about Jennifer's pedigree. Everyone in this town knows who's who and how they are related. It's the reason I escaped.

"Her grandfather was a McAleer! Related to your Uncle Christopher. A distant cousin, mind you, so you don't have to worry if you are too closely related." Her tone makes me regret my question. As expected, she takes her job of making sure she knows the family history seriously.

"I'm sure she is a nice girl, Gran," I say, wanting to end this conversation. *I don't want a nice girl.*

"Well, you won't get over that trollop without finding someone new." Trollop? Is that even an expression anymore? Yes, fine. I admit she wasn't my best choice for a partner, but at least our sex life was a lot of fun. She seemed to know my weakness, a good girl who says yes. Until I caught her with Josh. I pulled up anchor and split so quickly I left most of my stuff behind. I live at the fire station, so she knows where to find me. When she arrived one day to see if I would take her back, she didn't like my answer and made a scene in front of my crew. Screw her. When she threw the ring at me, I thought.... freedom.

Freedom to where? To do what?

"I think you should, " I cut Gran off and ask her if she finished today's puzzle. Maybe it's how we get off this maternal lecture of what I should and shouldn't do.

"You can't distract me, Andrew. I'm here, and you are here... you will listen." Oh, damn. That didn't work. I think I made it worse.

"Yes, Gran."

"Good Boy," she says as she starts into what kind of girl will be best for me so I can settle down in Mountmooke Bay and give her great grandbabies for her to enjoy. I zone out, looping back to the 'good boy' comment. *Is that what I am?* A good boy? I doubt it.

I feel like I'm lost at sea and can't find the shore. I am not what she expects, but I refuse to show her my confusion and lack of direction when it comes to finding a partner.

There is no one I want.

There is no one for me.

There is no one... yet.

I try to pull in the positive thoughts and think about who my ideal woman might be. *On her knees and wanting more.* I smirk. "Are you listening!!" I sit up straighter, knowing I'm caught. *Damn it.*

"Sorry Gran. I know this is important, but I wanted to tell you about the bathroom reno," I say, trying to change the subject.

"Oh!! Did you get the grabby things in for me?" she says, now off the topic of my love life. Thank goodness I can usually distract her with the house she loves so much.

"Yes, the grab bars are in, and I took some pictures to show you," I say as I open my phone. I notice there are a few messages from my Aunt Christine. I swipe them away, thinking I'll look at them later.

As I open the album called 'Gran's renos', I let her take my phone and flip through what she wants. I created an album, knowing she needs to hold the device and review it at her leisure. My main photos have some 'not for Gran's eyes', and I couldn't risk her swiping to see those. Since some women found out about my breakup with Britt, they have been sending me some pics. The one I got last night was very nice, and I saved it, knowing I could use it for my pleasure later. Britt might have stomped on my heart, but my dick doesn't understand, and he needs attention.

As Gran flips the last of the photos, she asks about the chair installation. "I'm meeting with the chair guy later today," I say. She hands me back my phone as I repeat the plan for her 'fancy' chair that will take her from the first to the second floor of the house.

"Well, I want to see the options before anything happens," she reminds me.

"Yes Gran, I promise. I will bring you pictures and the quote later today.

"And cupcakes?" she asks, as a grin breaks across her face.

"Yes, I will sneak you in some cupcakes."

"Thank you, my sweet boy."

"I better head out," I say as I go to stand and feel another text vibrate from my phone. Aunt Christine... again.

"Okay, say goodbye to Jennifer on your way out," she says as she glances down and adjusts her blankets.

"Okay, Gran. I'll see you after supper."

"With my dessert!" she says as I kiss her cheek and turn to go, unable to hide my amusement. *I think my matchmaker will be just fine.* I realize I can play along, the doting grandson who remembers I will do whatever she wants.

As I stride down the hall, there is no sign of Jennifer, and I'm a little curious if she could be someone to bridge the gap until I find my good girl to settle my restless soul. I look at the five messages from Aunt Christine.

Are you at the hospital with your grandmother?

I'm coming in an hour to see her. Will you be there?

Did she tell you about the scan? Don't do too much to the house before we talk. I'm not sure if she'll be able to move home.

Call me when you can, please.

DO NOT get her sweets! Her sugars were too high this morning.

Good lord. How does Uncle Christopher put up with this whirlwind of a woman? I reread the 'not sure if she will be able to move home' again. I brush it off and think good luck telling Gran what she can and can't do.

There is no way I'm not coming back with those cupcakes. Gran will never forgive me. I smile, thinking about how happy it makes her and isn't that the point? Joy at seventy-five through cupcakes. Aunt Christine must be overreacting about the sugar thing. A hint of doubt creeps in. Maybe I should check?

3

CALL ME DREW

CHARLEY

I stand for the last hymn, realizing my mind might have wandered during the sermon again. Damn. I hope Margaret doesn't ask my opinion about anything. I wait patiently in my pew and watch as she makes her way through the crowd, smiling at her church community friends. She likes to sit in the second pew. Maybe if I sit close, my mind will stay focused like hers.

I wonder what she will ask me today. Rev. McInnus's views have usually sparked some friendly debates, but over the years, I have tried not to be so controversial. Our friendly conversations feel more like a pop quiz every Sunday. Lately, I've been doing remarkably well with my answers, which seems to please her.

Margaret was the first person I met when I moved into my little bungalow in The Grove fourteen years ago. When I saw the 1940s cottage was for sale, I knew it would be a bit of a leap for me to own my own home as a single mom with a two-year-old, but The Grove seemed like the perfect place to raise a child with a community that seemed to invent neighbourhood watch. There was a rumour the previous owner died in the house, so it sat on the market forever, with the price continuing to drop. A tragic circumstance ultimately turned into an unexpected stroke of fortune for me.

One of my friends saw the For Sale sign and suggested it was the best way for Troy and me to get out of the third-floor walk-up downtown. "It's no place to raise a kid," she said. At first, I took offense because I thought she was passing judgment, but I should have known better. She was a good friend who always looked out for me, too bad she moved away, and we lost touch.

The day we moved in, I met Margaret, and I will never forget the first thing she said to me: "Finally, some fresh faces in this part of town. This is how I stay young." It swept away any doubt I had about my decision.

Her husband passed before they had children, and since she never remarried, the community was her family. She seemed to have a soft spot for Troy from day one, becoming the extended family I so desperately needed. Eventually, filling the gap of the maternal grandmother we were both missing.

The low hum of conversation pulls me back to the present moment. As I watch her move down the aisle toward me, I realize how this small-framed woman has carried so many of my burdens over the years. I wonder if she'll be able to shoulder the weight of my latest worries too.

"Hello dear," she says as I move to her for an embrace. She smells sweet with an earthy undertone that makes me grin. It means she was working in her garden before service, and it's likely soil is still clinging to her dress.

"Wonderful service," I venture.

"Yes… " She trails off as she sees another friend who grabs her attention. I continue to shuffle with her toward the door. It's slow today as we wait for everyone to shake Rev. McInnus' hand and tell him how much we loved his sermon. I used to think this was a strange tradition, but now I can't imagine it any other way.

Margaret pats her friend's hand and takes me by the arm, tugging slightly to tell me to come closer. I lean down, curious to know what she wants.

"I noticed Troy didn't make curfew last night."

"Why were you up so late?" I glance at her as we continue to take another step forward, but I already know the answer. She doesn't sleep either when he isn't home. Troy would probably say he has two mothers who need to mind their business. *But you are my business, mister!*

"I think you need to bring him with you next Sunday. Drag that boy here. He can sit with me, just like he did when he was little. Do you remember?"

"Yes, I still haven't figured out how you kept him so well-behaved."

"Magic Margaret," she winks.

I had forgotten the beloved nickname. *I could use some magic now.* "You are coming over later today? I want to show you how well the clematis is doing on the east side of the house," she says as she beams with pride.

I am more than happy she remembers how much it means we still have our Sunday afternoons together.

Since Troy hit his teenage years, it's like a weekly therapy session. Sometimes, she can judge my mothering choices a little too sharply, but I cherish the wisdom of her eighty-eight years.

"Yes, of course," I say, kissing her cheek.

She reaches to shake Rev. McInnus' hand, praising his take on sins of the flesh. *Sins of the flesh! Maybe I should have paid more attention.* He is very pleased with her comments and seems to let me get away with a 'thank you Reverend lovely service' comment as I hurry behind Margaret out the door. I might not do very well on Margaret's quiz today. I've been hiding my sins of the flesh from her this long. There is no need to reveal them now.

I help Margaret to her car since she insists she can drive to church. "Three left turns and a right," she chimes as I close the door for her and make sure she has buckled herself in.

I'm grateful she only has a short distance to go, but she needs this level of independence despite how much I worry she will get home safely.

"And I will see you in about an hour," I chime back. The reassurance of our Sunday routine is oddly comforting; I try not to think about the day it might end.

She slowly pulls out of her spot, and I wave even though I know she has her eyes on the road. I only turn away after I've watched her slowly turn onto the street. I glance at my watch and think if I head to the spot on Wilson for a quick grocery run, I can be back to see her as promised.

"Charley!" I hear a high-pitched voice calling after me, and as I turn, I see it's one of the regulars, but I can't place the name.

"Hello," I say, moving closer to her, hoping the proximity will lower her voice and bring less attention to us.

"The strawberry social is on May 31st, and I want to put you down for two dozen scones. Can you do that dear? We all must work together to make this year as successful as last year," she says in a sing-song voice with a slight midwestern accent. I note the hint of being *voluntold* in her request.

"Yes, of course. It's not a problem. Do you want them by nine o'clock like last year?" I ask, relieved I remembered what I did last year. I don't want to disappoint or get blackballed as 'one of those women who doesn't help when our church needs them'. I've tried my best to do whatever is required; just please don't put me in charge.

"Oh, wonderful! Thank you, Charley." She squeals a little in delight. I don't know how anyone could get so excited about scones.

I drive into the parking lot of SuperGrocer (whoever came up with the name needs a reward for how many chuckles it creates) and shoot a text to Troy.

I hope you are up and have cleaned your room.

I'll be home in 30 minutes. I'm just stopping to get the groceries for the week.

yes, mother

UGH!

He knows he's grounded for missing curfew last night. But calling me *mother* is his way of showing a little sass. I wish I didn't have to always play the bad guy with him. It would have been easier if his dad was still in the picture, but *he* ran off with Missy when Troy was still a babe in arms. She seemed to understand the importance of his baseball career better than I did. I put my phone in my purse and decide I will not engage in another argument with him, especially not via text.

The grocery store is busy today as I try to navigate the narrow aisles with my cart. It has one wheel which keeps catching. I take a brief inhale and try to put my best face forward. It is a beautiful day, and I should not let things I can't control ruin it. My cart is half full, and I know I am missing some items. *Where did I put my list?*

I pull my purse from around my shoulder, and the slight movement seems to stretch my floral dress and makes me uncomfortable. Maybe I should have gone home to change. The dress might be appropriate for church services, but here, I feel out of place. I straighten the bodice and notice the third button-down is barely hanging on. *Well, damn it. Don't breathe; you'll release the girls.*

I turn my cart around, barely missing a display of rice on sale. I take a deep breath, trying to calm my nerves, and my stomach lurches at a smell I can't identify. I need to get out of here. *Why did I think this was a good idea?* I reassure myself that I can stop after work tomorrow. As I round the end of the aisle, my cart plows into another shopper.

"Oh, my goodness! I'm so sorry." The person I ran into, or should I say wall of a man, doesn't seem fazed as he stands holding a box from the bakery section. His smirk eases my embarrassment.

"It's okay, miss," he hesitates. "Charley?"

"Andrew!! I didn't even recognize you!"

"Well, it's been a few years. How are you?"

"I'm umm," my cheeks flush, trying to figure out how to answer his question without spilling all my problems onto this man who I haven't seen since high school. The boy, who seemed to be more focused on having fun, never had a steady girlfriend despite the line-up waiting for him to notice. I was in the line, and no... he never noticed. *But he just said my name. How does he know my name?*

I was just a silly teenage girl the last time I saw him, and now he's a wall of muscle that sends a rush of heat through me at the thought of him in his firefighter uniform.

Oh, my god. I notice his neatly trimmed beard around full lips, smirking at my awkwardness. Can he read my thoughts? *Speak!*

I swallow, trying to find words. My mind flashes, remembering Martha had a fall and was hospitalized. "I heard your grandmother was in the hospital. I hope she is doing alright."

He looks at me with a 'how do you know that look?'

I answer quickly, "My neighbour is good at keeping me in the loop about the ladies at church."

He nods as I observe his body's subtle movements, unsure if he is comfortable with me knowing about his business. You can't live here without most people knowing about your business. "And your grandmother comes to the bookstore where I work," I add. "Is she doing okay?"

"Yes, she sent me to get these cupcakes for her." He motions to the box. "I'm heading back there now."

"Well, maybe you can tell her Margaret says hi? She would want me to pass the message."

"Yes, of course." He nods, a slow smile forming on his face.

My throat feels suddenly dry. He's not what I remember from high school. *I need to get a grip.*

High school Andrew and this man in front of me are different. Eighteen years will do that to anyone. *I'm not exactly the same girl.*

"I'm sorry about hitting you with my cart. I wasn't paying attention. I should be more careful," I say in a way that feels awkward and too apologetic. "It is nice to see you again, Andrew," I say as I push my cart toward the cashier.

"It's Drew. You can call me Drew," he says as he lets me pass.

Drew.... why does it sound so sweet coming from his lips?

I nod in reply. I want to ask why he shortened his name; he was always Andrew in school. But I bite my lip to stop the questions from tumbling out. Maybe

Margaret will know. I glance down at my bodice, and the third button has left me. My eyes look up at Drew to see if he noticed.

"See you around, Charley." I hear as he walks away. *Maybe he didn't notice.*

I pull my dress together awkwardly, trying to be subtle, knowing there is no way to hide the gaping hole which exposes the bottom of my bra. I leave the cart, telling the boy who is restocking the cantaloupe that I have an emergency and I'm sorry I need to leave my cart of groceries here. I don't even stay long enough to ensure he understands as I pull my purse to my chest and race out the door.

Of all the days to have that happen. *Maybe he's curious, and he wants to see more.*

I start my car and head for home. My thoughts drift to the many questions I have about Drew. Will I ever get to see him again? I don't know if I can wait another eighteen years.

～∞～

4

MARGARET'S ADVICE

CHARLEY

I changed so fast out of the dress, filled with the shame of my interaction with Drew.

You should have given him your number. Oh gawd, I'm mortified. Well, at least now I don't have to worry about wondering if we ever had a chance. *Sigh.*

I walk past Troy's room and notice he is sound asleep, likely still recovering from his nighttime shenanigans, and I'm not waking him to get him to eat. He will not be pleased there's no supper, since I didn't get any groceries.

I leave a note on our communication whiteboard, 'gone to Margaret's'. It is more of a mom board, since he rarely leaves me a note, preferring to text. I feel a brief twinge of guilt about the food situation and add, 'love you'. Maybe this summer will be easier since he's playing baseball for the Dolphins. Maybe I should just go to one of the big grocery stores in Ridgeport and stock up the freezer with food he can grab on the go.

Maybe... Maybe... Maybe.

I sigh again, opening the door to Margaret's back porch, noticing how comfortable Miss Camilla looks in her lap. Some days, I wish I was a cat and could relax like that.

"Hello dear! Did you talk to Troy?" Margaret asks.

"He was sleeping. I didn't have the heart to wake him." It's a small fib, and she knows it, as she looks at me over her glasses.

"Well, he came over when I got home from church. Almost like he was waiting for me."

"Really?" I say, unsure where this is going, but my curiosity is getting the better of me.

"Yes, we had a right smart chat after he apologized."

"He apologized?" Unable to hide my surprise, I hope she will continue to fill in the blanks for me.

"Yes. I told him how tired I was for staying up worrying about him. How my heart can't take such stress?" She explains as she continues to pet Miss Camilla, and I can't help but feel like she is holding court today as the details unfold.

I continue to nod and let her explain. Interrupting with questions will only annoy her. She has always had Troy's best interests at heart, even if we don't always see eye to eye.

"He seemed to be hungry, so I gave him some meat pie, and he just scarfed it down like he was starving. Poor thing," she says.

Poor thing? I continue to nod, encouraging her to continue. *He is not starving. He is a bottomless pit, and she knows it.*

"It seems he had an issue with his friends and a girl. He stayed until he was certain her father came to get her. Seems our boy has a protective side."

"That's why he missed curfew?" I blurt. Damn it, now I feel like an ass. I should learn to ask more questions.

"Yes, but I'm not sure I believe it yet. I will do some asking around to make sure he isn't fibbing; you know how I hate fibs," she says as she stands, disrupting Miss Camilla's nap.

"You stay put; I'll get the tea," I say.

"Thank you, dear. We have so much more to discuss." I nod and head to the kitchen. I agree with her; we do have so much more to discuss. I feel like some days, we need to make an agenda, so I don't forget all the items.

As I make the tea, I prepare the tray with the linen cloth decorated with blueberries that she loves so much. The tea set was a wedding gift to her and her husband. It took almost a year of us doing this Sunday ritual before she trusted me with her prized possession. I asked her once why she used it if she was so concerned it would break. "Because what good is having something if you don't use it, dear". A lesson I have learned well over the fourteen years I have known her.

We've grown closer since her heart attack in 2009. I thought we were going to lose her, but she proved she was determined to get stronger and make sure she was around to watch Troy become a man. Her husband died young, and I think she has decided she wants to die old in her 1940s cottage house surrounded by her gardens. It makes me hope that someday I get to be strong like her when I'm eighty-eight.

I finish the final preparations before carrying the tray, which includes checking where the cat has decided to lie. Checking my path, not wanting to be tripped on my way into the back porch. Margaret's house is a challenging obstacle course between the little stools and throw rugs she insists on keeping. It all screams 'fall risk' to me, but I know my reasons are selfish and more for me since I have likely fallen more times in her house than she has.

"Here we go." I set the tray down on the small table between our chairs. It's the perfect size, and the little girl inside me who loved to play tea party smiles inside each time I do it.

"Oh, it's lovely, dear," Margaret claps her hands, scaring Miss Camilla, causing her to dart under the chair.

"Oh, you are fine Miss Camilla. No need to get all upset," she says. I pour the tea and ready myself for the questions about Rev. McInnus' sermon.

The conversation flows easily, and I navigate the questions better than I expected, even though I know I don't remember everything he said. Margaret doesn't seem to mind how I answer a question with a question to keep her talking. I smile and admire how such a woman can find joy in the simplest pleasures. Conversation over tea.

After we finish our second cup, which is the signal our visit will soon end. "Oh, I forgot to tell you I saw Andrew Stanton today. I remembered how his grandmother, Martha, was in the hospital and told him to tell her you said hi. I hope you don't mind."

"Andrew is home?" She asks.

"Yes, you don't mind. I mentioned you said hi?" I say, circling back to the question.

"No, no. That was very kind for you to remember, dear. One of the ladies is taking me to see her tomorrow. But I didn't know her grandson was home."

"Well, I went to high school with him, and I almost didn't recognize him," I say. I don't want to admit how I literally ran into him with my grocery cart.

"I heard he was engaged, " she pauses. I hold my breath, wondering if she will continue. "How did he look?"

Yummy.

"Fine. He was getting cupcakes for Martha."

"Oh dear, Christine won't like that. She's always on her about her sugars. I'm glad it's not a worry for me," she says, taking the last cookie from the tray.

I want to put the tray back in the kitchen and clean up for her, but I'm anchored to my seat, feeling desperate to learn more about Drew and his family.

"Well, it seems like he was getting it because Martha asked, but what do I know?" *Why am I feeling defensive all of a sudden?*

"No worry, dear. Andrew does what he likes, no matter how he presents himself," she says. My eyebrow rises, wondering what her statement really means.

"You know the family well?" I ask. *Simple question, but do I want to know the answer?*

"Just a few things over the years. Martha has four grandchildren; Kevin is the one I would choose for my daughter," she says. She doesn't call me her daughter, but I know the hint she is dropping. *Dare I pick it up?* Her husband passed before they could have children, so I've been happy to be her surrogate daughter slash neighbour for many years. The role comes with all the perks and less drama.

However, I wouldn't even know what to compare it to, especially after my mom moved to France with her new husband. I refused to go with her, determined to figure things out on my own at seventeen. Our relationship was already falling apart, and when I told her I was pregnant, she didn't handle it well. Who knows where she is or what she's doing now? It's not like she's made an effort to reach out since. I never knew my father, and anytime I tried to ask, she'd shut me down fast. That's a wound I don't need to reopen right now.

Focus.

"Kevin is Drew's brother, right?" I say, trying to remember any minor detail so she will continue to give information. "People talked about how he was so smart and went to some fancy school."

"He went to Harvard Law dear," Margaret corrects me. *Is she trying to make her point about how Kevin is the better brother?*

"Andrew took off to Colorado. I'm not sure why he had to leave so quickly. Maybe if he was here, things would have been different."

"Different?" I say, unable to stop myself. I know it is not her way to gossip outright, but this tactic is frustratingly slow.

"That's for another time dear. I'll see Martha tomorrow and get a better idea of how things are going. I'm sure Andrew won't be here long. You likely won't see him again."

I hope that's not true.

"Well, if your friend can't take you to see Martha tomorrow. I can drive you," I say, secretly hoping maybe I will get to see Drew again. "I know you don't like to pay for parking, so it's no bother," I say as I stand.

"That's kind of you dear. You can just put it on the cupboard," she gestures to the tray I'm now holding. "Actually, my cousin Michael is coming to town for a visit. He said he'll take me."

"Oh, that's nice. You haven't seen Michael in a while." I say, searching my brain, trying to remember the last time I saw him. *A year?*

"Don't worry about that, dear; I can put it all away. You go check on Troy. Make sure our boy is okay." She winks at me. I can't help but smile.

"Miss Camilla, come here pet," she calls out and I see the cat under the chair and flick her tail in response.

I take everything off the tray and place it beside the sink so she can manage the cleanup easily. I know even if I clean the pot, she cleans it a second time to make sure it's done right. Maybe someday she will see I've passed her cleaning test. Or maybe it comforts her to cherish the items which bring her joy.

"You know that boy, Andrew," Margaret says as I head back into the porch. I hold my breath, unsure about what she will say next. "I know you said you went to high school together, so I don't know how well you know him."

Not as well as I want to.

"Not really. It was a long time ago." I say, trying to reassure her even though I'm not sure why.

"I think his engagement ended poorly, although I don't know all the details," she says. But what do you know? "So, I think he just needs to be left alone. From what I've heard, he's more handsome than his brother, but he seems to carry a lot of pain with him."

Pain? Well, her words only made me more curious. If she was trying to make me stay away, then she failed. *Don't confess that.*

"Well, you don't think he will be here long. I'm sure I won't see him again."

"Yes, thanks for hearing me out Charley. I don't want you to get mixed up with an old high school chum who needs more than you can offer," she says.

What does she mean? I don't dare ask more questions because I'm sure it will not give me the answers I seek. "Thanks for the chat, Margaret. See you tomorrow before supper?" I ask as I lean down to kiss her cheek.

"Of course, dear."

As I open the gate and head to my backdoor, I wonder how one conversation could make me feel such a mixture of curiosity and confusion. *Who is Drew now? And why does Margaret want me to avoid him?*

This makes no sense. *Well, hopefully, we can wipe him from today and focus on the workweek ahead.*

Or maybe he will appear in my dreams... those shoulders... the forearms. Damn it, I'm screwed. She might as well have pointed me in his direction. *Why do I have to be so damn curious?*

She must remember the last guy I dated... fiasco. It started out nice, but then what a disaster. Troy hated him. I should have read the signs. It seems my inner dirty girl has a mind of her own, and she is blind to men with baggage and commitment issues.

Maybe Drew is different... *maybe.*

5

FUSSPOTS AND NICE GIRLS

DREW

I sit listening to the man explain the types of chairs that can be installed in a home. I feel like I'm in a bad sitcom as he quips jokes, trying to cover up the aggressive sales pitch. "Isn't that what your grandmother deserves?" he says as I ask why the extra lumbar support cushion is worth $500 extra. He throws back his head in a laugh which makes his sparse hair wave a little out of place, so he has to smooth it down as he resumes his explanation.

"The 207 model has a smoother ride. No worries, she will bump along as she navigates the chair," he says.

"Is that even a concern? Maybe you shouldn't have a chair which bumps along," I mutter.

"We can have it installed in four hours, and I have openings next Tuesday," he says, ignoring my comment.

"I will let her know," I say, gathering the brochures with the prices written on each model. "I'm sure she will call you if she has questions."

"Do you want me to reserve the afternoon?"

"Not right now, thank you." *I have to get out of here before I say something rude.* The bell of the main door chimes as I leave the store in Ridgeport. I'm expected to be at the hospital in about an hour and since I'm only thirty minutes away, I decide to take the scenic route back to Mountmooke Bay. I haven't driven the route in years, and I could use the time to think. I glance at my phone before I leave the parking lot, and I see I have two missed calls from Aunt Christine. *Damn it.*

I press the call-back button and put her on Bluetooth as I head toward Highway 12. "Hi, Aunt Christine, I'm sorry I didn't call you back right away. I've been running around."

"No worries, Drew. I heard you were heading to the assistive devices shop in Ridgeport?"

"Yes, I got all the information for Gran. Didn't decide yet. Figured she can make the choice."

"Well, you know your grandmother well," she says. "I called you because I want to talk to you about the renovations at the house. I know you are working so hard. I just am concerned about getting too much done."

"Too much? What do you mean?" *What is she talking about?*

"We can talk about this more in person. Are you driving? Are you alone? Maybe it's not a good time." I turn right at the stop sign, noticing there seems to be some congestion at this intersection. *Pay attention to the road.* Am I on the right road?

"Yes, I'm driving, and I'm alone. Just tell me, Aunt Christine. Are you worried she doesn't have the money to cover the renos? I can help. I want her to have what she needs to be independent in the house." I say as I stop at a crosswalk to let a man and a small child cross safely. The little boy is skipping, and the man is encouraging him to cross quickly. I smile, thinking how sweet it is, and my heart tugs... will I ever have that in my life?

"Your grandmother is fine for finances; I'm helping her with her banking, and she's always been frugal. No worries in that department." She says, pulling me out of my thoughts and back to the issue at hand.

"So, what is the concern then? Can you tell me what is going on?" I ask as I accelerate to the speed limit and head out of the city. I should see the signs for the highway soon.

"She had some tests and is now scheduled for some more. It's not confirmed one hundred percent yet, but I am concerned her cancer might have come back." She pauses, waiting for my reaction.

Well, that sucks. I'm silent.

"It's not for sure, and I don't want to worry you too much. I know you have a lot going on." She adds.

"How bad is it?" I ask.

"What? Pardon, Drew? I'm sorry I can't hear you. Oh dear, I must have lost you."

"HOW BAD?" I say, raising my voice and leaning forward, thinking the Bluetooth microphone must not be working. *Where did they say it was installed again?*

"Oh! There you are!" she laughs. *LAUGHS!* This is not a laughing matter, Aunt Christine. *Just tell me what is going on!* I pull over on the side of the road.

"I've stopped the truck. Please tell me the details," I say. A pause. Too long of a pause. "Aunt Christine?" nothing. Then I hear the radio come on.

Damn it. I lost her.

I pull back onto the road and see the sign for Mountmooke Bay, twenty-three miles. It's time to get back. *I hate phones.*

I dial again. It goes to voicemail. *Damn it.*

I turn off the radio so I can think. This is why you wait and get news face to face. This over-the-phone stuff is too stressful. I sit in silence with my thoughts to keep me company, figuring out a plan to get Gran home. I know that's where she wants to be. I can help. I can do this for her. I have eleven days left of my leave of absence, plenty of time to figure this out.

You need more than eleven days.

I dropped everything for my mom. If this is what Gran needs, then that is what I will do. I can get on with the fire department in Mountmooke Bay. *They should hire, right?*

Everyone is always hiring first responders. I take a deep breath to calm my racing heart. *If not, I can work at SuperGrocer.* I can learn how to stock shelves or do whatever it takes to be home for Gran. *Whatever it takes.*

Maybe I will get to see Charley again. My mind relaxes as my thoughts wander in her direction. The road is now a steady stream of vehicles heading westward. The landscape is opening in places so I can get glimpses of the river that will lead me home.

Home.

It hasn't been my official home in so long, but maybe it's time for me to call Mountmooke Bay home again. I wonder if Charley has always called it home. Did she go away after high school like so many of us did? There weren't many jobs back then, so it created a mass exodus of young people seeking to make their way around the world in bigger cities. I left for different reasons. After Kevin and I sold the house when my parents died, we moved in with Gran to finish school. Kevin only had a few months left, so we shared the one little bedroom upstairs. Not daring to complain, just happy we didn't have to stay in our other house with the memories. *And the nightmares.*

It was always the same. I'd be in the kitchen, and Dad would come in through the back door, injured and asking for help. Then he'd collapse, his legs giving out. In each version of the dream, he'd say something different before dying in my arms. Those nightmares finally stopped when I moved in with Gran.

Now, I'm back in that same room, all set up like I never left. *No need to go anywhere else,* she said. *It's still your room.* She hasn't changed a thing since 1996. Then again, I never come home long enough to bother changing it myself.

Part of me finds comfort in the small bedroom. The smell of cedar from the closet Gran lined to keep out moths still lingers, mixed with the sharp scent of Old Spice aftershave. That smell clings to everything, ever since the bottle broke near Kevin's bed. We were arguing—something petty—and I snapped at him for wearing Dad's scent. I didn't mean to knock it over, but the bottle shattered, and the aftershave seeped into the floorboards. You'd think after all these years the smell would fade, but it's still there, etched into the wood, into my memory.

Dad's presence is now woven into the house.

I kept more of my mother's things. She had moments of lucidity during her hospitalization, and we talked about the things she liked. I brought things to her to help her remember on the days her brain seemed to misfire. Desperate to have her make the connections and come back to us whole. After three months of tracking her thoughts, I got well-versed in how complicated the brain recovers. *Until it doesn't.*

"Love you, Mom," I say into the cab of the truck with only the hum of the tires. "I miss you."

I see the sign telling me I'm only eight miles away. I try Aunt Christine's cell again. Voicemail. What was she going to tell me?

It feels like only a short few moments before I'm parking at the hospital and heading up to the third floor. My bag of Gran goodies was in one hand with cupcakes, two new puzzle books and the chair brochures. I mentally check the list of requests and I'm fairly certain she will be pleased.

I notice there are some loud voices coming from room 302 as I pass. "This is for your heart, Mr. Wallace."

"I don't want your stupid goddamn pills." A male voice shouts. Who I'm assuming is Mr. Wallace. I smile to myself, wondering if that is how I will be when I'm older. Stubborn.

I open the door to 308 and see Aunt Christine there with Gran, helping her into a chair. "I got it! I got it! I'm fine. Stop fussing!"

More evidence that I likely got my stubbornness from the Stanton side.

"Well, I just want to make sure..." Aunt Christine says.

"Drew!" Gran interrupts her 'fussing' with a little swat to Aunt Christine's hand. "I'm so happy to see you."

"I'm here Gran," I say as I lean in to kiss her soft cheek. How is her skin so soft at her age?

"Do you have everything I asked for?" Gran asks.

"Yes, do you want to look at the brochures first?" I hesitate. Silently hoping she won't ask about the cupcakes. I can't afford to have Aunt Christine mad at me right now. She might not share any information if she knows I'm not following her orders.

"You have a look at the brochure. I'll be back in a moment. I want to see the nurse before she finishes her shift." Aunt Christine grabs a notebook and heads toward the door.

"I think she was in with another patient," I say, wondering if I'm being helpful to my aunt.

"Oh, did you see Jennifer?" Gran asks with a slight lift of her chin.

"No, I just heard someone trying to help a gentleman in room 302." I wave off the question, and Aunt Christine takes her leave, unconcerned that who she wants to talk to might be busy helping someone else.

"How are you?" I say turning to Gran, watching her straighten the blanket around her legs. Hoping we can change the topic to important matters for just the two of us to hear.

"I'll be better when you fish out the cupcakes. I can smell them from here."

"You can? Well, don't tell Aunt Christine. She already warned me not to bring you sweets."

"Oh, hush, child, she is such a fusspot." She says as I place the bag on her lap. "This is our little secret." *What other secrets do you have, Gran?* I want to ask so many questions, but I decide to let her enjoy her sweets.

"Good?" I ask.

She nods approvingly.

"When I was at SuperGrocer to get them, I ran into someone who told me to tell you Margaret says hi," I say, reviewing the sentence in my mind, wondering if it makes sense.

"Oh, that's nice. Margaret is supposed to come and see me tomorrow. Maybe you can meet her?" She asks between bites. "Who was it you saw if it wasn't Margaret?"

"A girl I went to high school with. She says she knows you too. She works at the bookstore on Harbour Street. Charley?" I say, hoping my thoughts about Charley don't show on my face.

"Charley? Yes, she works at the Harbour Street Booknook. She's so good at keeping aside my favourite authors." She grabs another cupcake from the box.

"That's nice of her," I say, taking the box and hiding it back in the bag. No need to wave this secret in front of Aunt Christine. I'm sure she'll be back at any moment.

"Yes, she never left after high school. Poor thing had big plans to go to college, but everything changed when she got mixed up with Nick Fletcher. You remember him?"

"Yes, I do," I say, holding back the thought: *He was an asshole.* "How do you know all of this?" I ask, curiosity pushing through despite the bitterness lingering in my mind.

"Margaret and I have been friends a long time and Charley lives next door. Like a daughter to Margaret since she moved in with her son. He was a little boy back then; I think he's sixteen now. Nice girl. Margaret and I were on a mission to get rid of the last boyfriend she had. He was awful! Even Troy didn't like him." She tells me as she peels the paper from her cupcake. I want to tell her to eat it quickly, but I know she is savoring the last bites.

"Troy? She has a son?" I ask, surprised Gran is sharing so much. *Is she gossiping or warning me?*

"Yes. Nick didn't just walk away from the relationship—he left her with a child when he went off to chase his baseball dreams. Signed with some coach, thinking he'd make it big. She claims she hasn't heard from him since, or at least that's what she tells Margaret. Honestly, I think she's better off. Troy's never met him," she says.

"Never met him..." I repeat her last words as they hit me like a slap in the face. Nick. Once an asshole, always an asshole.

"They did fine without him. They have Margaret, and she has them. A family they made from necessity and stays together because of... " She takes her last bite, not finishing her sentence, and I notice her eyes go wide.

"MOTHER!" Aunt Christine says as she marches into the room. "What did you just shove into your mouth? Is that a cupcake?"

"Nama upin," Gran says through a full mouthful, and I have a hard time not laughing.

"I gotta go," I say. I need to escape this confrontation, although I'm sure I'll hear about it later.

"Ugh, what is the point? Just have the sweets, Mom. Enjoy!" Aunt Christine says in the most resigned, sarcastic way imaginable.

"I'll come back in the morning, Gran. We can look at the brochures later," I say, kissing her cheek as she continues to chew. Nodding and smiling at her success.

"I'll walk you out," Aunt Christine says. *Damn it.*

As we head toward the elevator, there is an alcove with some chairs, and she motions for me to have a seat. I feel like I'm twelve years old and in trouble for failing a test. *You failed the test. You didn't follow the rules.*

"I'm sorry, Aunt Christine. It's hard for me not to give Gran what she wants." I say, sitting up straight in the chair. Why am I so nervous around this woman?

"Well, the sweets are one issue, Drew, but we need to discuss what I was trying to tell you on the phone today." She says, and I realize maybe I can finally get some answers. "Your grandmother will have a new round of cancer treatment. I've set it all out with the doctors, and I want her to come and live with me. It will be easier for me to manage everything if she is close by."

"Pardon?"

"It's all been decided. I'm putting Gran's house on the market and making a spot in the back room at my place," she says, reminding me of my dad. So strict and determined. Will not bend to anyone else. The decision was made, and no one will change her mind. Must be a Stanton thing.

"Does Gran know all of this?" I ask.

"Not yet, so I need you on board. I'll tell her tomorrow, and I want you to help her see this is the best for her." Aunt Christine straightens her back, finding renewed strength with getting this all out in the open.

"Well, this is all very sudden. I understand you will do what is best for Gran. I want what is best for her, too. Can I be here when you tell her?" I ask.

"Yes, that would be a great idea. Can you be here for 9 am?" She asks. I nod in agreement, and it feels like a business transaction. I wonder if my cousins are as intimidated by this side of their mother as I am. I need to think this through. I have so many questions, but I feel like she will only feel threatened if I say much more. I stand to leave, feeling the push to be out of this space immediately.

"I'll see you tomorrow, Drew," she says with a sigh. "And no more cupcakes, please. Oh, never mind. Let her eat what she wants." I feel the heaviness in her voice, and I turn back towards her. She looks tired, weary that one good night's sleep likely can't fix. I lean down and give her an awkward hug that is more of a pat on the back. She isn't an easy one to take affection. *Poor Uncle Christopher.*

"I'll see you tomorrow," I say, leaving her alone with her thoughts. I can't get out of here fast enough. *So many questions.* What kind of cancer? What treatment? Will she be okay? Why sell the house? Charley has a son!

I open my Facebook app on my phone. I'm not great at posting, but maybe Charley is? I find her easily. 'Charley Jane Thomas'. The boys used to make fun of her and call her plain Jane, but there is nothing plain about that woman. Her profile picture is of a young boy in his baseball uniform. He looks like he is eight years old. Young, so young... must be an older picture. Didn't Gran say he was sixteen now? How old is she?

I click on the 'about' button and see her birthday is on February 16, 1979. One year younger than me... I was right. Satisfied with my search and not wanting to creep her any longer, I go to swipe out of the app. *You should send her a friend request.*

Now, THAT would be stupid. I start the truck and head back home, but will it be my home for much longer?

6

THE BOOKNOOK

CHARLEY

I look down at the stack of books in the crook of my arm. I've been wandering about the store with them for a while, unsure of where to display them. Not that I am in a terrible rush. I've not had many customers this morning, which is typical for a Wednesday. I read on days like today. It's slow, so I might as well catch up on my TBR list.

I'm reading a new mystery by a local author, Caroline Tucker. We have a book signing in a week, so I better know what it's all about before the event. Caroline likes to quiz me on minute details, not that I mind. She brings in good business for Mrs. Mahone, the owner.

Today, I can't seem to get lost in the book. My eyes drift over the same paragraph again and again, but the words slip through my mind like water through a sieve. It's as if my head refuses to escape into her world. *Because I'm too caught up in my own.*

Troy has been extra helpful around the house, so I lifted his punishment this morning. He seems to have learned his lesson about missing curfew. I didn't tell him I knew the details about why he was late, and he didn't offer the information about how wanting to help this one girl who needed to wait for her dad. I admit his actions softened me a bit. I guess I shouldn't be so harsh on him. He is growing up so fast, and he'll be off to college before I know it.

I decide to rearrange the main table to create a cozy romance display. It's almost June, so maybe it will bring in some sales as people decide which book to buy for their holiday this year. I clear the table and set out in my mind ideas for the new display. Maybe I could borrow some of Margaret's vases for some flowers? No, the petals might make a mess. Some beach items from the SmartSave? No, my boss won't want to spend the money. Maybe I could go to the beach and get some shells?

The debate whirls around my head as I stack and arrange the table. I hum to the tune on the radio. Usually, it's turned low, so it doesn't bother the customers, but today I need the company.

And if you call, I will answer...

I survey my work. What's missing? Oh, yes, the Emily Millar series. Perfect! It will fit across the back. She has a new book coming out soon; I continue to hum, pleased with my progress.

And if you court this disaster, I'll point you home...

I find the books I need, and I feel the shift in my body. I'm relaxed. I'm in my happy place in the stacks, remembering I don't need many adventures in my life. I only need books. The smell, the textures. I sing.

Now it's time to prove you've come back here to rebuild. Rebuild, REBUILD!

I belt out the fifth rebuild as I round the corner.

Drew stands in the doorway. He's clapping. "Barenaked Ladies?" he says as I hug the books closer to my chest. I nod and try to find my voice.

"Yes... umm you startled me," I confess.

"Just when I thought you couldn't blush anymore, Miss Thomas," he says as I walk to the table and put down the books.

"Sorry, I thought I was alone. Didn't even hear the chime for the door." I guess I really was in my own world. "What can I do for you, Drew?" I say, heading to the main counter to turn down the radio.

"I saw them in concert once," he says. "Small venue. Outside. It was amazing."

I can't help but stare at him. This man is full of surprises. I didn't expect him to recognize the song, and the fact that he did leaves me feeling off balance. I want to ask more, but I need a moment to catch my breath.

He must notice my discomfort as he edges closer. "I'm sorry I startled you. You have a nice voice," he says, putting his hand on the counter and leaning slightly.

"Well, now I'm going to be beet red. So embarrassing." I shake my head and try to laugh it off. "I never sing in front of anyone."

"Why? It seems like it makes you happy," he says, handing me a slip of folded paper. I am glad about the distraction. I don't know how to explain my singing out loud issue is related to my mother's harsh words about how it gave her a headache.

"What is this?" I say, opening the paper to reveal a list. "Oh! This is for Martha. Of course. It is the third Wednesday of the month. She never forgets." I smile.

"I guess not. She said you would know what to do. I'm on orders to hand you that and wait."

"Wait?" I ask. Usually, she gives me a day to gather the items she wants to read. I glance at the list. "This shouldn't take too long. Want to have a seat?" I gesture to the chair near the window.

"I thought I could help you?" His shoulders rise in a simple, innocent gesture that tugs at my heart. Why is this man affecting me like this?

"Well, let's head this way. She wants something by Jane McIntosh, lets head to the romance section," I say, leading the way. With him close behind me commenting on how many books we stock here.

"The owner, Mrs. Mahone, has been in business since 1971 and loves to collect forgotten books," I say. "Roaming the stacks can be an adventure all on its own."

"I can imagine." His breath comes out heavy, and I turn to see how close he is behind me. Did he just sniff me? *You are imagining things.*

We consult the list a few times and I'm only able to find two of the six books on Martha's list. It is the most fun I've had with a scavenger hunt since God knows when. Each time I reach for something, he gets excited and reads the title out loud.

"Here is one!" he says and tries to read the back of the book in a British accent. Laughter bubbles out of me, and he adds it to the pile. *What was that?*

"Who would have thought Gran liked the happily ever after sappy stuff?" he says as he trails his finger down the spine of another book. *I wish he'd trail his finger down my spine.* Focus!

"I don't know your Gran well, but I know her taste in books," I say, pulling another option off the shelf. I quickly put it back, realizing I have the wrong one. Heat rises in my cheeks.

"Let me see that one," Drew says. "One Night of Passion? Well, now, I think I need to read this one for myself." *Is he flirting?* I go to grab the book back, but he swipes it away, flipping through the pages.

"The font is so small; give me your glasses," he says, squinting at the text. *He's trying to be funny.* I remove my glasses from my head, and they are tangled in my hair. Not the best place for them, but I only need them for distance, so I put them there out of the way. *It's a bad habit.*

"I don't think these will help you," I say, handing them to him. He takes them with a sweeping gesture and perches them on the end of his nose. I giggle at his antics. Definitely trying to be a funny man.

"Well, thank ya kindly. Now, what do we have here—aaah?" His exaggerated southern drawl, dripping with charm, pulls a laugh from deep in my chest.

"Oh, my stars, I can't read a single thang," he teases, handing the glasses back, his fingers lingering just a moment too long against mine.

"Always the comedian," I say, sliding the glasses back onto my head, but my heart races, and it's not from the joke. "They're for distance." His antics leave me flustered; I entirely forget what we're supposed to be doing. *No customers, I haven't heard the bell.* But somehow, being alone with him is the only thing on my mind.

"Well, I still want to read it. Looks interesting enough," Drew says, adding the book to his small stack with a grin. I shake my head, amused by his enthusiasm.

We continue browsing, lost in conversation, until I finally think to ask him the time. When he checks his phone, reality hits—nearly an hour has passed. How does time slip away so easily with him? Being around Drew makes everything else fade, like the world bends just to keep us in this moment.

"I think that's all I can find today; I'll keep searching for the rest tomorrow," I say, leading him to the front of the store.

"Well, I think she has enough to keep her entertained for a bit. And I do, too." He winks. I blush again, hoping he will like it and maybe we can talk about it later. Discuss the 'One Night of Passion' and see what he thinks. *Of all the books I pulled off the shelf today, I had to pull that one. Maybe it wasn't an accident.*

I don't want to tell him I've read it a few times. A hot, steamy romance between two people who meet on vacation.

He is about to leave when he turns back toward me. "I have to pay you for these. How much do I owe you?"

"Oh no, Martha and I have an agreement about books. I'll settle with her next month." I'm sure he wonders what I mean, but I won't give away our book exchange secret. I have the same secret with a few friends of Margaret's from the church. They love books too, so we have a little lending library set up for them. Most of the bookstore is made up of used books, so the owner, Mrs. Mahone, encourages the arrangement.

"Well, it was nice hunting books with you, Charley," he says, the slight hesitation in his voice making it clear he's not quite ready to leave. *Do I shake his hand? Hug him? Pat him on the head?* My brain freezes, and I feel awkward, like I'm stuck in a rom-com with no clue what the script says next. I want to see him again... there's something about him that draws me in, like we're just getting started. But then Margaret's nagging voice pops into my head: **Stay away.** Seriously? Why? I don't get it. What's so wrong about wanting more?

"I better get these to Gran; see you around Charley," he says, reaching for the door, but his hand is knocked away as it flies open, and Troy barrels in.

"Mom! My cleats! I forgot them in the car," Troy says.

"Oh, dear," I say, heading to the main counter to get my purse with my keys. I look. It's almost four o'clock. I turn back, and notice Drew is waiting patiently. *He didn't leave.*

"You have a bit of time before practice. How did you get here?"

"Thomas drove me," he says, grabbing the keys. "Thanks Mom. Be right back." He races out the door to the parking lot. He knows where I park the car. I've used the same spot for years.

"Sorry about that," I say to Drew. "That's my son, Troy."

"Yes, I gathered that. He's so..." he doesn't finish the sentence before Troy is back in, handing me my keys and thanking me again.

"One second, mister." Troy stops with his hand on the doorknob. "Be home right after the practice, no later than seven."

"Yes, Mom," he says with a sigh as I approach him.

"And this is my friend Drew. Drew, this is my son, Troy."

"Nice to meet you." Drew holds out his hand to shake, balancing the books in his other arm.

"Nice to meet you too," Troy responds and looks at me with the 'can I go now' look.

"See you later," I say.

He is out the door before he can hear me whisper, "Love you."

"Nice kid," Drew says.

"Well, teenagers are a challenge sometimes, but I try my best," I say, hoping he doesn't hear the exasperation in my voice.

"I'm sure you are... " His voice trails off, and I catch something in his eyes. *An unfinished thought?* I want him to finish his sentence. The air between us feels different, heavier somehow, like there's something we're both not saying, a question hovering in the space between us.

"Until next time," he says with a small smile, opening the door.

I watch him walk away, feeling an unexpected pull to chase after him. *Why do I want him to turn around?* I glance down and realize I'm still holding the book list, so I grab a pen to note which books we found. Three out of six. Progress, I guess. As I fold the paper, something catches my eye. Tiny numbers scribbled along the side. How did I miss this? It's a phone number. His phone number? A slow smile spreads across my face. Maybe I didn't imagine that unspoken thing after all.

7

THE SPARK

CHARLEY

I had a dream. I was tracing my finger along Drew's back, and a tattoo appeared. A beautiful blue and red Superman crest, but it wasn't an 'S' but an 'A'.

I keep going back to the dream and wondering what it means. Andrew? Maybe I should google dream interpretation. *Maybe I should just call him.*

I have been debating this for three days, but what if it's not his number? It's saved in my phone under 'mystery man' in case it pops up. I look around the café and take another sip of my latte, so delicious.

Okay, time to write. I need to get some inspiration for this story. I look at the screen of my laptop, mid-sentence and the cursor blinking at me, waiting for the next word to be typed. Inspiration... where do I get some inspiration? It's Saturday, time to create. I'm in my favourite spot at the Dragon Café, my weekly ritual. It's never been a problem before. Why now? *Drew... think about Drew.*

A wave of motivation hits me, and I can't get the words out fast enough without making a lot of spelling mistakes. Oh well, I'll fix that later. *His hand slides up my thigh, as I pant with anticipation....*

Part of me is hesitant, thinking it might be a challenge to write this story in public. I look around, and there's a line of people waiting for their coffee order. Extra busy today with people getting their caffeine fix, which helps me feel more concealed in my little corner. My favorite spot is by the window, which seems to be the best spot I've found to spark my creativity. I saw it in a show once about how an aspiring writer wrote in a coffee shop. I thought it was a bit cliché, but after hitting a few roadblocks at home, I gave it a shot. And it worked.

Saturdays at the Dragonfly, my routine. Instant access to the best coffee in town, and no one seems to bother me as I type away. Troy thinks I meet friends for coffee. He knows I like to write stories, but he doesn't know what kind of stories. *Smut, my son. Your mother writes smut.*

I savor another sip of caramel gold before continuing my description of what foreplay with Drew would be like. A deep ache stirs at the thought of how much I would relish the physical contact of a man. It's been so long. *I want to tell him how much I want his touch, but only a moan escapes my lips....*

The sentences form into paragraphs, and then, before long, the story has taken shape. I smile to myself. Proud of how my imagination can run wild with the thought of Drew. Drew... I wonder if he is still in town. *You should call the number.*

I've talked myself around this circular argument so many times, and it's always the same conclusion. If he wants to give me his number, he wouldn't be so obtuse about it. The paper is still in my purse. I've not had any luck finding the last two books for Martha, so I tell myself I'll keep the list in case I am somewhere and need to refer to it. *Liar.*

Why put the phone number so small up the side of the page? It still makes no sense to me. I look at the cursor on my screen again. MOVE! Write something. Anything. *Not like you have a deadline or anything.*

No, but writing is therapeutic, and maybe someday someone will be interested in reading my stories. To be a published author... I can dream.

I take the last sip of my coffee and look to see if I can get the barista's attention for another. He seems run off his feet today; I can wait.

I stare out the window, formulating the next few lines. *As he thrusts himself into me...*

No, it doesn't sound right. I pull my glasses from where they're perched in my hair and scrub my face, trying to refocus. By the end of my writing sessions, my hair is usually a mess from running my hands through it. I notice the hair tie on my wrist and debate tying it up now to resist the temptation. Instead, I smooth it the best I can and gather it over one shoulder. Glancing at the ends, I realize I need a trim. Maybe I'll do that tonight.

I stare at my screen again, wondering how to write about how it would feel for Drew to be inside me. How do I write the level of desire that explains the wanting? Maybe I need to pick another person to imagine. It's not like Drew is available.

You don't know he's unavailable.

I type again, just getting the words on the page and knowing I can edit later. Maybe if I get this out of my system in this way, I'll stop thinking about him.

You need your itch scratched. That's the problem.

The words take shape on the page as a fresh wave of inspiration washes over me. *The way he holds my hands above my head as he enters....*

My thoughts are interrupted by a fresh cup of coffee placed at my side. I'm on a roll and a little annoyed at Tom's timing as my fingers fly on the keyboard. I barely glance up from the screen to say, "Thanks, Tom." I should be more grateful that he took a moment to come over to make sure I had more caffeine. I will give him an extra tip today for my rudeness at half ignoring him.

"You are more than welcome." That is not Tom's voice. My eyes don't want to leave the screen, but I know that voice.

"Hiiii.... yaaaah," I say as I finish typing the word 'stroking'. Is my face turning red? *Yes, let's start that again.*

"Hi, Drew." I shut my laptop, fearing he'll see the words on my screen.

"Don't stop on my account. I didn't want to interrupt you, just looked like you needed a refill. Tom told me what you like," Drew says as he stands beside the table, holding a to-go-mug. *Don't be rude.*

"I can stop for a moment for a refill. Thank you, that is very kind. Would you like to have a seat?"

"Sure," he says as he pulls the second chair around, so he is sitting closer to my left knee. It's a tight squeeze between tables, so he sits at an angle. I wonder if it's common for him to have to maneuver furniture to fit his stature. He looks good today in his light grey t-shirt and jeans. I realize he doesn't wear logos when I've seen him. I wonder if it's intentional.

I scoot back from the table, adjust my pants, and cross my legs, trying to look casual, even though I feel his eyes on me. I pick up the cup and take a long, glorious sip. *Heaven.*

Coffee might just be the only thing saving me from blurting out, 'I was just writing a sex scene with you as the main character'. Instead, I play it safe.

"So, how's your grandma doing?" I ask, mentally congratulating myself for not going with the more scandalous opener.

"She's fine, but I'm about to head back over there. Needed a caffeine boost first. Dealing with her and my aunt is like watching a tennis match, back and forth, back and forth. I swear, if I don't get actual whiplash, I'm sure I'll at least need a stiff drink afterward." He chuckles.

I snicker, imagining him ducking for cover while his grandma and aunt volley insults over his head.

"I don't mean to pry, but Margaret told me your aunt wanted her to sell the house. I'm sorry, I'm not sure if I'm supposed to know that. I know Martha was pretty upset about it, and Margaret is on her side," I say.

He sighs and takes a sip of his coffee.

"I figured she would tell her friends. She's been very upset about it all, and to be honest, I feel a little stuck in the middle." He sighs, and I feel the weight of what it must be like for him. He seems tired. *I wonder if he goes back to work soon.*

"Anyway, I don't need to burden you with all my problems. It's been a long week, but I have a plan to bring her home on Monday. She is determined," he says, and I see his efforts to make the best of the situation.

"That sounds nice. And just so we're clear, it's no burden at all. Maybe I'll let Martha be the one to break the news to Margaret?" I ask, leaning forward just a little, testing the waters.

"Yes, I'd appreciate that. Gran will definitely want to tell her herself." His voice softens, and there's something about the way he says *Gran* that makes me want to ask a hundred more questions. But I hesitate—maybe it's not my place. He called it *home...* What does home mean for him?

Before I can dig deeper, he glances up at me, a flicker of uncertainty in his eyes. "Is that too much information? I mean, considering we don't know each other that well?"

"Yet," I blurt out before I can stop myself. The word hangs between us, and I immediately regret how forward it sounds. I bite my lip, silently cursing my lack of filter.

But then he laughs. A deep, rough laugh that seems to come from somewhere genuine, and his shoulders drop, relaxing for the first time since we sat down. "Don't worry about it. I like it. Your honesty is refreshing."

I smile, feeling a warmth spread through me. "Sorry, I just say whatever pops into my head. It's a bad habit."

"Don't apologize. It's... charming." His eyes linger on mine for just a second longer than they should, and suddenly, the air is charged. The hairs on my arm rise as if I've been shocked.

"I've noticed that about you, Charley. No need to hold back on my account," he says, his voice teasing, sending a flicker down my spine. I bite the inside of my cheek to keep from blurting out something embarrassing, like how I've been dreaming about him. Get it together, I tell myself, trying to rein in my wandering thoughts.

Instead, I latch onto something safer. "You said *home*. Is that where you're staying? Your Gran's,

Martha's?" I ask, hoping he'll keep talking. I want to know more about him. Maybe even bring up the phone number he slipped me.

"Yes," he says, nodding slowly. "I lived there for a few years after… " His voice fades, and he looks at me, waiting—almost like he's testing me, seeing if I'll finish the sentence for him.

The silence stretches, and I feel the weight of it between us. I lean in slightly, sensing the opening. My curiosity pushes past my caution, hoping he'll trust me enough to keep going, but knowing he might need to know, I remember.

"After your parents had the accident. I'm so sorry Drew. I don't know if I ever had the chance to tell you how sorry I was when we were teenagers."

"It's okay. I forgot you would know what happened. I rarely talk to people who know."

"We don't have to talk about them if you don't want to, but I remember. Mostly, I remember you missing a lot of school," I say.

"Ya, I had to do summer school to catch up. God, that sucked." He removes the lid from his coffee cup and takes a sip.

I see the steam rising off it. How did he not burn his mouth? I wonder.

"I like it hot," he says.

For a moment, I'm curious if he's reading my mind. I tilt my head, not a frown but definitely questioning.

"I could see from your face you were wondering."

"Am I that easy to read?" My cheeks flush slightly, betraying me.

"Pretty easy," he says with a smirk, and I bite my lip, pulling it inward to keep the flood of words inside. Does he have any idea how much he's making my heart race? It's like every word he says ties my thoughts into knots.

Part of me wonders what he would think of my stories. Of *him* in my stories. But before I can spiral any further, he gestures toward my laptop. "What were you working on?"

I glance down at the stickers covering the case, a collection of memories and inspirations gathered over the years. My favorite, a phoenix, stands out. I got it from an author who talked about how writing transformed her. It's always reminded me of how much I wish I could rise like that. Be my own phoenix.

"Pardon?" I ask, blinking up at him, unsure if I heard him correctly over the buzzing in my ears.

He grins, his eyes catching mine. "Charley why are you blushing?" he teases, and the heat in my cheeks deepens as I try to think of a way out of this.

"I, I don't. No reason." *Liar.* "How long are you staying in town?" Change the subject. Yes, I must change the subject.

"I took a leave of absence, not sure when I'll go back. I don't want to leave Gran just yet," he says before taking another sip. A gulp. Gulping hot coffee. Who knew that was a thing? Maybe it's a firefighter thing? No, it is likely just a Drew thing. "I'm not in a rush to go back. Maybe we could hang out some more?"

"Sure," I say, wanting to take that back. *Sure?? Just SURE?* You need to be more engaging.

"What do you have planned later today? Can I take you for a late lunch after I finish my check-in at the hospital?" he asks.

"That would," I swallow, trying not to show the emotions on my face. "That would be nice, but Troy has a game today. I try to watch all his games. Morale support and all."

"Oh yes, he enjoys baseball like his dad?" he asks.

"Yes... how do you know about his dad?" I say, trying to hold in my emotions. *Oh no, don't panic. He doesn't know the entire story. No one really does. Do they?*

"Sorry, I didn't mean to worry you or upset you. I remember Nick from high school," Drew says, leaning forward, his hands gripping the table as if he's bracing himself. His closeness should settle me, but my heart races. Calm down, I tell myself. There's no need to read into this.

But does he know the full story? How Nick chose baseball over fatherhood. I'll never forgive him for it, even though I've tried to shield Troy from the truth. He doesn't need to know what he's missing.

The thoughts stir something deeper. A raw anger, I hate to admit, is still there. People know the basics, but the rest. It's too painful, too humiliating to share with anyone. I've kept that part of my history buried, protective of Troy and protective of myself. Nick didn't just reject me; he rejected both of us. It's a burden I never wanted Troy to carry.

"It's okay. I try not to think too much about Nick" I shrug, wanting to tell him more about Troy but unsure how.

"I'm sorry for bringing him up. I can see it still affects you, even after all these years. I won't mention him again unless you want to talk about it," Drew says, his voice low and filled with a kind of reassurance I didn't realize I needed. The weight of his words settles over me, and for the first time, I wonder what it would be like to talk about Nick. About how the hurt never really healed, about the cracks he left behind.

But before I can gather my thoughts, Drew shifts. "I just went through a breakup," he admits, catching me off guard.

"Oh?" I try not to sound too surprised. It's not that I didn't know. Small-town rumors travel fast but hearing it from him in this moment feels different. Why is he sharing this now?

"Yeah, Britt and I were supposed to get married this summer," he says, running a hand through his hair before letting out a bitter laugh. "Came home early one day and found her in bed with another guy. She thought we could have a threesome."

He laughs again, but I'm stunned, staring at him, unsure of how to respond to his brutal honesty. The room seems to shrink as I try to process what he just said. Part of me wants to laugh with him, to shake off the shock, but another part wonders how much her betrayal must have stung. He's hurt, too, just in a different way.

"Ya, she was pretty wild, and she thought that would be a coverup for her infidelity. It didn't work. Josh can have her," he says with a wave of his hand, and I notice he's glancing around the café. I don't think anyone hears him, but you never know in this small town. Big ears are everywhere.

"I'm sorry, Drew. I didn't know the details. Margaret told me she heard you ended your engagement but didn't know why," I confess.

"No one knows. I've told no one. I'm not sure why I'm telling you now," he says as he sips his coffee again. The steam is no longer there, and it looks like it's a reasonable temperature now.

"Why are you telling me?" I ask.

"I just have a feeling you'll keep my secret. Will you?"

"Yes, I can keep your secret," I say. *All of them.*

"Thanks, Charley. I better head out," he says, standing with an effortless grace, given his size. As he pushes his chair back, the sleeve of his t-shirt rides up, revealing the edge of a tattoo on his upper arm.

Before I can stop myself, the words fly out. "What's that?" I blurt, pointing at his arm. *Tactful.* I mentally shake my head at myself.

He's not fazed, just grins as he lifts his sleeve with his left hand, exposing more of the intricate design. "Got it over ten years ago," he says. The ink wraps around his biceps and triceps, dark shading playing against the warm sandstone of his skin. He flexes his triceps, making the image come alive.

My fingers itch to trace the details. Tattoos have always been a weakness of mine. Margaret's voice rings in my head. **Stay away**.

"It's St. Florian," he says before noticing my confusion. "The patron saint of chimney sweepers, soap makers, and firefighters."

"Soap makers?" I raise an eyebrow.

He chuckles, his eyes twinkling. "I thought about taking it up as a hobby."

I laugh, and the tension between us lightens. His casualness, his calm confidence. It's disarming. He doesn't offer more, leaving me curious, and I mentally note to google it later.

He downs the rest of his coffee and tosses the cup in the garbage before turning back to me.

"Oh, before you go..." I begin. I want to ask him to sit down again so we can talk more, but I know his internal clock is telling him it's time to get to the hospital. "Can you tell Martha I am still looking for the last books? I don't want her to think I forgot."

"I already told her, but I'll remind her," he says, but there is a pause as he takes a small step toward me, forcing me to raise my chin to look him in the eyes. The movement makes my breath catch. The way his body can block out the other customers, creating a barrier so only I can hear him.

"I have another secret," he says, and I blink, my heart giving an unexpected flutter. I swallow, eager to hear what could come next.

"Gran put my phone number on the book list I gave you," he confesses with a sheepish grin. "She was hoping you'd call, thinking it was hers, but it's mine. She told me yesterday after she grilled me on why I hadn't heard from you yet. She has a way of interfering with my life that's... let's just say, not always appreciated."

I can't help but smile. "I noticed the number. It *is* yours?" I ask, digging into my purse, suddenly desperate to find the paper. *Where did I put it?* My hand dives deeper into the mess of receipts and stray items. *Where is it?*

"Charley, it's okay. Gran was just being Gran. I wanted to tell you myself, but now it feels awkward asking," he says, his voice calming me despite my frantic search.

"Ask me what?" I pause mid-purse-rummage, one hand still buried in the chaos and the other clutching random items that should have been put back by now.

He cocks his head to the side, that simple charm softening his features. "I was hoping you might give me your number. Maybe we could get together sometime?"

Yes, say yes. *Say yes!*

"Oh! Yes, of course." I shove everything back into my purse in a flurry, mentally noting I need to clean it out later.

He hands me his phone, and my hands suddenly feel clumsy as I type in my number. No name, just the digits.

He can fill that in. It's not the first time I've put my number in a guy's phone, but something about it feels different... more nerve-wracking like I'm teetering on the edge of something new.

I hand it back, and he glances at the screen with a quick smile. "Hope Troy's game goes well," he says, turning to leave.

"Thanks," I say as my phone buzzes. *Likely Troy.* I made sure his cleats weren't in my car this time.

"See you later." Drew walks away, and I can't help but watch as his jeans hug him in all the right places. God damn.

I glance at the chaotic mess in my purse, cringing at how ridiculous I must've looked during that frantic search. "There it is!" I announce a bit too loudly, causing another customer to glance my way. I give them a sheepish smile. Nope, not talking to you.

Relieved I've not lost Martha's precious list, I shove my laptop into my bag, glancing at my still half-full coffee cup. Great, I was so distracted I barely drank any of it. I take a sip, instantly regretting it as the cold coffee hits my tongue. I roll my eyes at myself and set the cup back down, wondering if there's a way to rewind the last few minutes of awkwardness.

I check my phone to see what Troy wants, and it's a message from 'Mystery Man'. *OH!!*

Hey, it's Drew.

I smile, typing my response.

Hi, Drew. Thanks for the coffee… and the company.

Anytime, Charley. I'm sure we could make a habit of it.

A habit, huh?

Some habits are worth keeping.

I stare at the screen, feeling the unspoken tension behind his words, a smile tugging at my lips. Friends, sure… but maybe a little more.

8

THOSE DAMN WIPER BLADES

DREW

It's raining. Not pouring, just enough of a drizzle that you don't need a coat, but you wish it would just dump and be done with it. *Let the sun come out.* The grayness of the sky dampens my mood more. What a day.

As I scan my parking pass to leave the hospital for the second time today, my arm gets wet, trying to get the reader to work. I was tired of paying each time, so they said I could get a monthly pass. Might as well, since she is not coming home just yet. *When will she come home?*

I feel like Gran has been here too long. I took her outside yesterday, determined the spring sunshine would be good for her. Good thing I didn't wait until today with rain clouds like this.

She started a new treatment this week, and they won't let her come home until she is more stable. It seems something about her liver is an issue. I don't really understand it all. I'm relying on Aunt Christine, but she seems to hold back some of the information. I'm determined to be part of the conversation.

Each day is basically the same. I visit at the same time to show Gran she can count on me and predict my schedule. Today I announced I was going to resign from the fire department in Denver. She was more concerned than I thought she would be. I expected her to be happy. *Doesn't she want me home?*

After a brief discussion on plans and how I would get my things, she agreed I could make her house my new home. Although it was very sweet of her, I told her it would only be temporary until I find my own place. *I need my own place.*

She said she wants me to stay there at least until she is discharged. "I feel better knowing it's not empty," she told me. Considering all the changes in the past three weeks, I am happy I don't need to look for an apartment right now. I made my bedroom downstairs in the back sitting room. It's bigger, and now I feel less trapped than in my teenage bedroom I shared with Kevin.

I feel like this new situation required me to let my position go at the station. I don't want to move back to Denver, especially with all the memories of Britt. It's time to make it part of my past.

When I called my captain to put in my notice, he was supportive, saying other departments will hire me. *I hope.* My record is excellent, and it should open some doors.

After settling my new living quarters and resigning from my job, it was time to deal with getting my stuff out of the old apartment. I texted Britt, refusing to talk to her on the phone. She agreed I could come this weekend. I asked her to give me some privacy as I packed up my things, but she texted back, saying she didn't trust me to be alone in the apartment. *Trust me? ME!*

My last text was requesting to pack some of my things, so at least I'm not there all day. I have little, but the faster I get my stuff and get out, the faster I can leave that life behind.

As I pull into Gran's, my house, I turn off the truck and sit in the driveway for a moment to collect my thoughts. Three weeks. That is all it's been. How much things have changed in three weeks?

My phone buzzes, and I see it's a text.

I need to get some new windshield wipers. Mine are awful. Any ideas on what kind?

It's been a pleasant change, these messages from Charley. She sends something almost every day. Little bits of humor that make me smile, like she knows I need it. *Maybe she does.* Lately, it's been hard to feel anything but exhaustion. Each day feels the same.

Hospital visits, and the sterile smell clinging to me no matter how hard I try to shake it off. It's like it's seeped into my skin and my clothes; no amount of soap will wash it away.

I sit in the truck, gripping the steering wheel, staring at the house. I should go inside, take a shower, grab something to eat. But the heaviness presses down on me, making it hard to move. I reek of hospital air. Of too much time spent worrying.

Just as I open the door, the skies let loose, and the rain pours down like a curtain. *Great.* The perfect excuse to sit a little longer. I watch the downpour, my mind wandering to Charley. The way she laughs, the way her messages light up my phone. I realize, despite the heavy days, it's her pulling me through.

My fingers hover over my phone. I should text her. Something to feel connected, to hear her voice. Even if it's just words on a screen. There's something about her... something that makes me want more than just these messages. I pull out my phone to answer Charley's text. Another one comes in.

Got some! The salesperson was a gem and helped me get the right size and all. I have an appointment to get them installed tomorrow. Only $50!

Hey, just got home. What was $50?

I see the dots appear and wait. The rain is soothing my mind, and I close my eyes for a moment. Maybe I could just have a little nap here to wait out the downpour. Bleep.

No, that's the installation fee. I just need to get an appointment. The salesperson gave me the number and said it's a good price.

No, that's not a good price. When are you home?

I'm home in 20.

I'll come and install them. Be there in half an hour.

Do NOT call that guy.

Damn the rain. My blood is boiling that she was taken advantage of at the store. What is wrong with people? I run inside, peeling off my wet clothes the moment I reach the bathroom. I need a shower, not just to wash off the stench but to cool down. As I'm about to step in, I glance at my phone and see her response.

Yes, Sir!

I smirk despite my foul mood. At least she listens well.

CHARLEY

Drew is on his way over. He's only been here once for the last of the books for Martha. He couldn't make it to the store in time, so I told him I would drop them off at the hospital. I thought it was a great idea. *Then I'll get to see Martha.* But he insisted he would pick them up, and I follow his suggestion even though I'm not sure about giving my address. I know Margaret will watch the exchange from her window.

Any movement in my yard, and she notices. I've always wondered how she does it so well. As soon as he leaves with the books, she is over asking all kinds of questions and giving me all kinds of warnings.

I try to reassure her I'm not interested in him romantically. "He's just getting books for Martha." I must say half a dozen times, but it doesn't work. She has warned me away from him every chance she gets. *Damn it.* Maybe I should tell him not to come. Margaret will be on my case again.

I'm not sure how much more she could be on my case about Drew. I pull my car into the garage so at least we will have a little privacy from her prying eyes. It's past five o'clock, and Troy is home. *What does she think will happen?* Drew is going to bend me over the hood of the car and take me right here and now? *Oh, yes, yes... let's do that.*

It's just wiper blades, I reassure myself. *Calm down.*

I try doing most things myself, but when it comes to my car, I get easily frustrated and give up fast. I will pay anyone to do car stuff. *Maybe I should pay Drew?* No, that's stupid. He is just being nice. I need to be grateful he's helping me. I'll need to see properly to go to work if it's still raining tomorrow. *One more thing off the list.*

I wait inside the garage to watch for Drew at the twenty-five-minute mark. He is early, so I'm happy to be ready as I hold the new blades in one hand and wave hello with the other. As he steps out of the truck, I see he's in jeans and a white t-shirt and his hat on backwards. *Drew's standard uniform.* How does something so simple turn me on? *Can Margaret see him? Will she come over?*

He jogs toward me, and his shirt is a little speckled from the raindrops. Part of me is happy he doesn't seem to be bothered by the rain or the extra droplets falling from the leaves of the trees hanging over my driveway.

"You are not!" He chuckles, coming into the garage. "You are NOT paying someone to install wiper blades!"

"Why? I pay for other stuff for my car." I say with a slight whine. *Is it only my ineptitude spurring him into action?*

"I can teach you how to do it if you like, but from now on, promise me you will not pay for car repairs before asking me first?" he says. *Asking him first?*

"You want me to run those things by you?" I ask, unsure if I understand him correctly.

"Yes, there is no need to spend money on things I can help you do, or I can teach Troy if you like," he offers. Part of me wants to dig deeper into this request. Is it a command or a demand? What is this? *Just shut up and say thank you.*

"Yes, Sir." I tease and give him a mock salute.

He glowers at me, and I can see he is fighting back words on what he wants to say to respond. "Wipers," he says, holding his hand out.

I hand them over like I imagine a surgeon's assistant would do if they said 'scalpel'. I watch him get to work, and I'm happy he is here, but I am not saying *that* out loud.

I fill the silence, telling him about the customers who came to the store today. I want to avoid questions about what he is actually doing. I have no desire to learn, although, from the ease of his movements, I realize I'm an idiot. He's making it look so easy. Part of me is embarrassed I couldn't do this myself, or that I thought paying someone to do it was a good idea. *It doesn't matter. He is helping. Just let him help.*

"Oh! I forgot to tell you! I had a dream about you a few nights ago," I blurt. *Is that the right way to change the topic?*

"I hope it was a good one." He keeps his eyes trained on the task before him, but I see the smirk forming and his attempt to control his thoughts and make a comment.

"Not that kind of dream!" I say, gesturing with a hand to swat him away. *What are you thinking to bring this up now?* I take a breath and realize there is no stopping now. I have to tell him to set the record straight. It wasn't a sex dream.

"I had a dream you had a tattoo on your shoulder. Not connected to your other one, but on the same side. It was red and blue, vibrant!" I say, excited to tell him the details.

He glances at me. "Interesting."

"Yes, it was like a Superman crest, but it was a capital A, not an S in the middle." I come toward him on the passenger side of the car as he is leaning over and touch his shoulder blade where the crest appeared in my dream.

I draw a crest shape and make an 'A' with my index finger to show what I saw. As my finger moves against the fabric of his shirt, I realize this is the first time I've touched him. He is solid muscle. My eyes move down his biceps, noticing its shape as he maneuvers the blade into the clip. My finger seems to have a mind of its own as it repeats the 'A' shape and moves the fabric of his shirt.

He stops and looks into my eyes. My finger stops moving, but it continues to maintain contact. *Stop touching him.*

"That's a weird dream," he says, turning back toward the windshield. I am snapped out of my trance, putting my hands behind my back. He tests that the blade is attached properly, and I take a step backward.

"Yes... weird," I reply. *Why do I feel so lightheaded?*

"Go turn on the car, and let's see if they work," Drew commands. *Focus.* The blades work perfectly, and I clap my hands in excitement.

"Thank you," I say.

"It's really not that hard," he says, as if it's supposed to reassure me.

"Well, I appreciate your help," I reply as he heads towards his truck.

"Anything for you." He smiles, but his voice trails a little. He turns and leaves abruptly as if he's forgotten something and must go somewhere else immediately.

I give a half-hearted "see you later" as I watch him drive away. *He left a little fast, didn't he?* I reason he has better things to do than hang around here. I guess it's better he was fast. Maybe Margaret didn't notice.

Did my dream upset him? Or maybe it was my awkwardness. *It was nothing. Don't overthink it.*

***

As I chop vegetables, my mind keeps drifting back to my last exchange with Drew. I thought he'd joke about it, say something ridiculous like, "I AM Superman!" or wish he could fly.

But he didn't. The banter I've grown used to between us just... wasn't there.

I stir the pot absentmindedly, glancing at the recipe, though I'm barely following it. I'll text him later to say thank you. Just get out of your head. It's probably nothing. But the doubt creeps, gnawing at me. Did I read him wrong?

I lift the lid off the pan, grimacing at the sight of the chicken. It's overcooked. *Great.* I try to salvage it, knowing Troy will probably eat it anyway. He's too hungry to complain, but I'm not sure if I'll be able to swallow more than my own thoughts tonight.

"Hello!!!" I hear from the backdoor.

"I'm in the kitchen," I answer Margaret's greeting. I would recognize her voice anywhere. It must be a quarter to seven. Her evening check-in is like clockwork. She eats earlier, and before she settles to watch her shows, she likes to come and say hello and have a sweet.

"Hello Margaret, how was your day?" I ask as she sits at the table in the kitchen, and I put the kettle on. The table is already set for supper, so I move Troy's plate over and set the teacup in front of her.

"I watched that rainstorm from the back porch, just hoping it was enough to give the hydrangeas a nice drink," she reports.

"Oh?" I say, setting three cookies on a dessert plate in front of her. I continue to move around the kitchen as she tells me about her garden. I wish I knew half as much about gardening as she does. She is so knowledgeable about how each plant reacts to temperature and moisture. I wonder if I should start taking notes. Maybe write a book, 'Margaret's Magic Garden'.

"What do you think, dear?" she asks.

"Pardon? Sorry, I think I overcooked the chicken. My mind is elsewhere today. My apologies." I say.

"Not to worry, dear. I was wondering if you might take me to Troy's game this weekend?"

"Oh! Of course. That would be lovely. I'm sure he would like to have more fans there. Did I tell you about the new uniforms this season?"

"Well, it hopefully will look better than those old black and red ones," she says.

"Actually, he isn't a fan of the new logo," I say as she takes a bite of her first cookie, and I pour the tea. "It's a cartoon dolphin balancing a ball on its nose."

"Seems a little childish," she says with her mouth half full and her dentures clacking. I should take her to the dentist again to get them adjusted.

"I don't know who chose it, but just say nothing when you see them. The colours are okay, a midnight blue with light blue accents."

"Oh, I won't say a thing, dear," she says. "Hopefully, he's only a Dolphin for another year. Then he can be called up to play with the Mariners."

"That's the goal," I say after turning off the stove. Supper can wait a moment. I need to rest my legs as I pull up a chair beside her. The comfort of this evening's routine is relaxing, taking away some of my earlier worries. She continues to drink her tea, and I wonder if maybe she didn't notice Drew's earlier visit.

"What time is the game?" she asks.

"Three o'clock, but I like to see warm-up, so can we leave here for two?" I suggest. Even though I'm in the throes of learning how to parent a sixteen-year-old son, I am very grateful Margaret is here to help me witness how he is growing up so fast. Another reminder that I don't need a domestic partnership. Our little world is plenty full, just the three of us. Troy doesn't need a dad, and

I'm secretly happy I've not had to navigate co-parenting with Nick. *But doesn't Troy need a male role model?* The hint of guilt still creeps in.

It doesn't matter now. He's almost grown. I am doing the best I can.

Margaret takes the last bite of her cookie and goes to stand. She is a little slower tonight to get up and I move to help her.

"Oh, it's all this dampness," she says to excuse her laborious movements.

"Yes, hopefully, it will clear in the night, and we can have sun the rest of the week," I say.

"Mom! Is supper ready?" Troy says as he enters the kitchen. "Oh, hi Margaret! I didn't realize you were here."

"Oh, hello, sweetheart. I swear you get taller every day," she says as Troy leans down to kiss her cheek. "How about you help me home?"

"My pleasure," Troy says as he holds out his arm for her to take. *Such a good boy.*

"I'll get supper on the table so you can eat as soon as you get back," I say.

"Oh, and Charley," Margaret calls out as they are crossing the threshold. "Maybe tomorrow we can talk about your visitor?"

I purse my lips and nod. *Why do I think I could get anything past that woman?* I go to respond, but Troy chimes in. "Oh, that was Drew. I met him at the bookstore. He just came to change mom's wiper blades," he says as he leads her out the door, grabbing an umbrella that seemed to appear out of nowhere.

How? What? Troy noticed too? I guess I can't do anything without these two knowing about it.

With them gone, I get supper plated and wait for Troy to return. I hope he didn't see me touching Drew. *The awkwardness.* I need to be more careful. We are friends. *Friends.* But... I hesitated when I touched him. *Damn it.*

I chastise myself for not being careful enough to keep my actions in check. *I think he noticed.* I blush as my thoughts veer into vivid images of taking off his shirt, and me tracing each muscle as he playfully tells me he came here for more than just wiper blades. *Bad girl! He's off limits! Your friend!*

Those damn wiper blades. Drew... I think you could get me into all kinds of trouble.

9

Coffee Delivery

DREW

I bolted. I fucking bolted! What is wrong with me? I park in the driveway at Gran's and am wondering if I should go back. I need to tell her how hard it was for me to control myself when she was touching me. Maybe not. Friends, we are supposed to be friends. God, I hope she didn't see how aroused she was making me. All cute and sweet, telling me about her day. And the glasses...

how do I not love the way she swishes up her nose to adjust them on her face. *Adorable.* I have to get a grip.

I go into the kitchen, focusing on getting some food into me. That's what's wrong with me. I need to eat. Maybe have a nap. Maybe jerk off. *And imagine how soft her lips would feel around me.*

As I pull open the fridge, the bottles in the door rattle. I see half a rotisserie chicken. That will have to do. I don't even grab a plate. Just dive in and start feeding the hole that seems to be in my chest. I need to satiate this hunger before I do something stupid. My Charley fantasies are starting to take over. She is always on my mind.

I head to the living room after devouring the chicken and flip on the television. Basic cable, not that it really matters since I'm not a TV guy, and there is a sitcom rerun on that will have to do. *Get my mind off Charley.* Maybe I should text her.

I look at my phone and see it's almost seven. Is she done supper? Do I reach out? *What is wrong with me?* This woman is turning me inside out.

I put my phone on silent, face down on the coffee table. Focus on the show. It's not working. I lean back and close my eyes. Maybe that's what's wrong. I need to sleep. Within moments, I can feel myself relax while the murmur of the TV is in the background.

***

I wake up slouched over, disoriented, and noticing the complete darkness outside the window. *What time is it?*

I grab my phone and see I have six messages. I open Charley's message, rationalizing that Aunt Christine can wait. She's likely just checking when I'm heading in tomorrow. It's the same every day, but something about our message routine is comforting in this unusual circumstance.

> **Hi, just wanted to say thank you for doing my wiper blades. I appreciate it more than you know.**

I look at the time, and she sent it at quarter after eight, almost an hour ago. *Damn it.*

Hey, sorry for the delay. I fell asleep in front of the TV. Not a problem with the blades.

I mean it tho, if you have more stuff to do with your car you can run it by me first. You shouldn't pay for things Troy, or I can do.

I open Christine's text and answer my usual response. I could copy and paste it from yesterday, but I type it out all the same. Another text from Charley comes in as I press the little blue arrow to send.

I will.

You rushed off pretty fast. I should have offered you something to drink.

Sorry about that, I was feeling hungry, so my stomach was making all the decisions.

Liar, it was your dick. Well, don't tell her THAT!

Snacks! I should have offered you something. My bad.

Next time, lol.

I wait for the next response. Do I ask her about going out to eat with me? She shot me down last time. *Maybe it's not such a good idea we do those things.* Maybe it's too much like dating, and we should steer clear of that option. In my impatience for her next text, I send her another.

Are you working tomorrow?

Yes, my regular 8-4 tomorrow. Shouldn't be too bad.

Would you like a coffee delivery mid-morning? I can bring you one after I have my morning visit with Gran.

Please say yes.

That would be lovely! Thank you.

I pump my fist in the air. *You are stupid.* It's only a coffee.

Great, see you tomorrow.

Night.

I need to see her and make sure the awkwardness between us is gone. Tomorrow is a new day, and things always look better in the morning. Refocus, regroup, and reestablish some boundaries.

CHARLEY

"I know Rev. McInnus. I appreciate you stopping in. Thank you." I nod as he turns to leave, "Can I help who is neck... next?"

Heat rises to my cheeks as the next customer comes to the counter. It's been a steady stream of customers today since Caroline Tucker's book signing. Seems many people are suddenly interested in her new book. She left me with fifty signed copies, and I'm down to twelve. I'm so distracted by Rev. McInnus and his list of requests that I don't notice the handsome man behind him. "Hi, I'm looking for Mrs. Thomas?" the tall gentleman asks.

"I'm her, I mean she." My cheeks flush scarlet as I hold out a hand for him to shake. Recognition filters into my brain. "Michael? Oh, I didn't recognize you!"

"Well, I think it's been over a year since we saw each other last?" he replies.

"At least. It's nice to see you again. Margaret told me you were coming for a visit. Where are you staying this time?" I ask.

"I booked a spot on Parkside near the golf club," he says. His hint of a British accent makes my heart beat a little faster. I recall how his quiet confidence and relaxed nature pulls me in. I wonder if he notices my nervousness.

Margaret has flexed her matchmaking skills with us in the past, but I've never admitted how I felt about him to her. He always feels a little out of my league, and I'm unsure if he would want to explore a relationship with someone like me.

"Margaret said you might have one of the first editions of Benson for sale?" he says, interrupting my thoughts.

"Yes, she told me you were interested and wanted me to look. I'm sorry I haven't found what you are looking for here. I have two third editions, but my guess is they won't do," I say, pulling out the books I put under the counter yesterday in preparation for his arrival. "I admit, I love a good book scavenger hunt, but Benson seems to be missing from our stacks. I'm so sorry."

He takes the books from my hands, brushing them with his fingertips. I notice their warmth. *He's never done that before.* He flips through the books and seems pleased with the shape they're in. "My copy is not nearly in such good condition. You have a very nice specimen on your hands. How much?" he asks, lifting an eyebrow. *He wants them?*

"Well, I'm glad you like it," I say, telling him the price. He hands me a fifty-dollar bill. I go to give him the change, and he waves me off.

"I'm going back to Margaret's later. Perhaps I will see you then?" he ventures.

"Sure, that would be lovely," I say, trying not to sound too excited. As he walks out, he holds open the door for Drew, who has two coffees in his hands.

"Thanks, man," Drew says as Michael nods and walks away. I notice Michael appears slenderer than Drew, who seems to take up the whole entryway. I blush again, thinking of those broad shoulders and the ink on his arm.

"Coffee delivery!" Drew announces; two customers who are browsing look up and look disappointed when they realize he isn't talking to them.

"Just what I needed. Thank you so much," I say as I round the end of the counter, and he hands me the cup with a cardboard sleeve. I look at the top. It's marked '1C' in black marker, a simple order, but he never fails to remember my morning coffee order is dark roast with only one cream. *No sugar; we are sweet enough.*

I breathe out a thank you as I take my first sip. The smell fills my nose before I can taste the bitterness I crave. I offer for him to sit, offering the stool to my right. He politely declines. "No, you sit. I'm sure you have been on your feet all morning. Seems busier today," he says as his eyes sweep across the room.

I perch on the high stool at the corner of the counter as I take another sip.

"It has been busier than usual. We had a book signing last week, and it seems to have drawn in some new customers." I lean in so I can talk in low tones and not disturb the lady who is reading six feet away. She has been there for over an hour and seems to be enjoying the story. I don't mind if she treats us like a library if she is happy.

Drew and I take a sip at the same time.

"God, that tastes good, thank you so much."

"My pleasure." He smiles and I know he wants to ask a question by the way he is now fiddling with his cup.

"What's up? Everything okay with your hospital visit this morning?"

"Yes, all is well. She has no treatments today, so I was happy to have more of a visit. It makes a nice change from the other days."

"That's good," I say as another customer comes closer to ask about a book I have on backorder. I take down her name and promise her I will contact her as soon as it comes in. She seems pleased. Her satisfaction makes me happy. I turn back to Drew; he is watching the exchange and waiting patiently.

"I just got to see Miss Thomas in action. Well, that's a treat," he says as I smile at him.

"I like to make sure my customers come back," I say.

He nods in agreement, looking at his cup like he is word searching.

I stay silent, knowing he will probably make some quip about him coming back but has bought nothing yet.

"You didn't blush as much with her as the last customer," he says.

Well, I didn't see that coming. "Pardon?" I take a quick sip of coffee before I blurt out anything else.

"Oh, nothing. No, I take that back. It's something because I see you are blushing now," he says as he takes another sip.

I'm not sure how to hide my embarrassment. "Was it that obvious?" I say a little too loudly.

"Yes, it was," I hear a customer say. The lady who was reading and now stands in front of us. "Sorry to eavesdrop. It was sweet to watch you get your feathers ruffled by that handsome man earlier. It was hard not to notice," she says.

I don't know how to respond as I glance at Drew. He just shrugs.

"I'd like to pay for this, please. Great read so far. I'm having a hard time putting it down," she says, getting out her wallet.

"That's great. Can I let the author know? She's local," I add.

"Even more exciting." She pays for the book, and I hand her the receipt.

I want to ask her more about what she noticed in the store, but my embarrassment tells me to be grateful for the sale and stop talking. As the bell on the door dings at her departure, I realize Drew and I are now alone.

"I'm so embarrassed," I mutter into my now lukewarm coffee. As if it will reassure me.

"Nothing to be embarrassed about," he says.

"Well, he's Margaret's distant second cousin or something like that. She tried to play matchmaker in the past, but he's not interested."

"Oh, no?" he asks.

"Well… I've not had much luck with her *suggestions*," I say, rolling my eyes. "She's always given it a solid effort to help me find someone."

Drew doesn't seem upset with my declaration, so I keep going. "I hope to find someone someday, but it's just so much work. All the men I've dated so far ghost me when they know I'm a mother of a teenager."

"Well then, they aren't the right kind of men," he says, trying to reassure me.

"You are right," I say, pausing for another sip of my coffee before it gets even cooler. "Thank you for bringing me this."

"Again, my pleasure. I hope you have a quiet rest of your day after such an exciting morning," he says.

"I'm supposed to go to Margaret's later. I'm sure she arranged it all so she could try to convince me to be with Michael," I say.

"Michael?"

"Yes, that's his name. The man who was here," I say, noticing Drew has also finished his coffee, so I know he will leave soon.

"Interesting. And she wants you to be with Michael?" he asks, but I feel there is a hidden meaning in his question.

"Maybe?" I hold the coffee close, hoping he thinks the flush of my cheeks is from the drink and not because of my inner thoughts. I feel my dirty girl pulse, and I tell her to be quiet.

Now isn't the time. Michael is influencing me in a way I don't want Drew to notice, but he's staring at me. "What?"

"What? Oh, I think you know what," he teases.

Is he calling me out on my attempt to ignore him? I take another sip slowly, prolonging the answer, hoping he will change the subject.

He stares at me, waiting patiently. *Drink your coffee and be quiet.* "Does Charley Jane Thomas have dirty thoughts she wants to share?" he asks.

"That's crazy," I say, biting my lip to stop the next sentence from spilling out. *He can tell you are lying.*

"Michael, eh? Interesting. That's my middle name," he says as he saunters toward the door. "I better go. Talk later?"

My thoughts screech to a halt. *My world is shifting.*

"Pardon me?" I ask. He stops, hand on the door. *Is he really leaving now when things just got interesting?*

"Well, maybe you can tell Andrew Michael Stanton about these dirty thoughts," he says, moving away from the door.

I move toward him, hoping he will come back inside to discuss this. *Did he just refer to himself in the third person?* He must be teasing. How many more moments do I have before he leaves? My head swims with all the new information.

What do I say next? Do I redirect this conversation? I am in dangerous territory. I don't know what to do. Thoughts flicker around my mind. I bite my bottom lip, not saying a word. *You want to share, don't you?*

"I... I better get back to work." I straighten the stack of books on the primary display.

He takes a few more steps toward me. "I'm sorry to tease you. You are just such an easy target. Every thought seems to show on your face. I'm sorry to embarrass you," he says. His attempt to smooth it over is not working.

I swat at him playfully. "You fiend," I say, trying to change my face, so it doesn't give away all my secrets.

"Have a great day, Charley," he says as he pulls the door open. The little bell rings, signaling his departure. Again.

Did I just open a door that I can't close?

10

COFFEE BREAK IS OVER

DREW

I didn't turn to look back at her, even though every fiber of my being wanted to. I quicken my steps to get to the truck to gather my thoughts. *What am I thinking?*

Putting the truck in drive, I head back to the hospital. Gran got her discharge notice. She comes home in two days, but I couldn't tell her after the Michael distraction. I don't know what that was all about, but as she told me, I struggled to try not to scream out my thoughts. *He doesn't deserve you!*

Why couldn't I just tell her what was on my mind? Because when she bit her lip, it sparked a need inside me, and I got distracted.

There was something about seeing her today—an unfamiliar twist in my gut that I can't quite shake. I pull into the grocery store parking lot, hoping that running through Gran's list of things to restock will clear my head. Anything to distract me from the thoughts swirling around Charley, but it's not working. The way she curls her hair around her finger when she's nervous keeps flashing through my mind. And today, the way she clutched her coffee close to her chest, fingers wrapped tightly around the cup, as if it would keep her steady. She seemed nervous, her body pulling inward, but all I could think about was how perfect she looked, how much I wanted to be the one to hold her instead.

I catch myself, my jaw tightening. This shouldn't be where my mind is, not now, not with so much else going on. But the thought doesn't let go. It lingers, heavy, as I stare at the store entrance, trying to push the image away. I should think about Gran, about the errands. Instead, all I can think of is how much I want to bury myself in Charley. There's no escaping it, no matter how hard I try.

I grab a shopping cart and start down the first aisle. *What the hell are you thinking, man? She is Charley! Not your fuck toy.*

I glance down at the list, skimming the vegetables. Cabbage? I wonder if Gran wants to make cabbage rolls when she gets home. The memory of savory garlic and simmering tomatoes fills my mind, instantly making my mouth water. God, I love those. Just thinking about it makes me hungry. Does Charley like cabbage rolls? Probably not. But then again, who could resist Gran's? They melt in your mouth, the tang of the sauce blending perfectly with the soft, seasoned filling.

Stop. Get her out of your head. I shake it off and focus back on the list, gripping the cart handle a little tighter than necessary. Focus.

I need to get ready for Gran to come home. I quickly check my phone, no Charley text. I shove it in my pocket and push the cart down the next aisle. Time to compartmentalize.

Good luck with that.

11

A New Boundary Explored

CHARLEY

Getting ready for work, I change my top six times. It still doesn't look right, but I give up. I reach for my big black sweater, pull off the accumulated hairs, and wrap it around my body. Now, I'm comfortable. It's late June, but the temperatures are still cool. No one will notice I'm covering my outfit; they'll just think I'm trying to keep warm.

My phone keeps dinging with texts from Drew. This is our new normal, pre-work conversations about the evening before and the day to come. We have skirted around the Michael issue from last week. He's been preoccupied after he was told Martha's discharge is delayed at least another five days. *Poor Drew.* I know he's worried about her.

I try my best to distract him with silly stories about customers and Troy's baseball game. The team are back to their old uniforms after the new ones shrank in the wash. Troy is relieved. He says it's embarrassing to have a 'stupid' cartoon dolphin on his chest.

Ding. Drew. I'll answer in a second. I glance in the mirror again before heading to the kitchen. What *is* up with my hair? I grab the elastic from my wrist and tie it up into a messy bun, grateful the bookstore doesn't care what I look like. It's not like anyone's looking, anyway.

Pouring my second cup of coffee, I finally check Drew's last text.

Did you see last night's episode? I was shocked when they revealed he went home to his wife!

Drew and I recently started watching a new show together—well, together, but not together. It's our thing. Something to talk about the next morning over texts. *Tell him you had another dirty dream about him last night.*

Nope, not doing that. I don't want to admit the episode shocked me. I'm not answering him as fast as usual. I'm still processing. The main character has a wife and kids, the total package. But he's cheating.

Why?

I take a sip of coffee and finally type back.

I just don't understand why he is doing that.

What could he be missing to make him cheat?

I don't even know if I want Drew's answer. *Do I?* A few seconds later, the screen lights up.

Maybe some men need more than one woman.

What? My eyes widen, and I nearly spill my coffee. I'm not sure if he's being serious or if this is more about the show.

Have their cake and eat it too, huh?

Maybe they don't have the right woman.

I stare at his response, my heart skipping. Is he talking about the show or… something else? My stomach flip-flops, but I push the thought aside. I've got to open the store in less than an hour, and here I am, spiraling over a text. I drop my phone into my purse. *Stop overthinking it, Charley.*

As I shove my feet into my sneakers, the question nags at me. *What does Drew really think about marriage?* The idea itches at me, pushing me to grab my phone again. *Don't do it.* But my fingers move on their own.

> **How do you think that could work in real life?**

Am I really asking this? My thumb hovers over the 'send' button for a moment too long before I hit it. I need to know what's going through his head. It's like I'm pushing him to say something I'm not sure I want to hear.

A moment later, my phone buzzes.

> **I don't know, but I think it's every man's fantasy to have a woman who can fulfil that need. Like that man's 'lady in the city'.**

I roll my eyes. Sure, he's still talking about the show, but there's something that makes my chest tighten. *Is this what men like Drew really think?* I don't know what to say, so I send a laughing emoji like a total idiot. *Very smooth, Charley.*

I stuff my phone back into my purse, but my mind is spinning. *Is this what men want?* Don't they want a wife? Or have I had it wrong all along? A flood of *what ifs* hits me hard. What if we're just programmed to believe in this one version of love? What if the traditional husband/wife thing isn't the answer at all? What if there's something better... something I can't see yet?

***

Thinking back to my time with Nick feels like revisiting a memory that starts sweet but turns bitter. I thought he was my forever, but we were just teenagers, clueless and overwhelmed.

Then I got pregnant. The timing wasn't perfect, but I convinced myself that somehow, we could make it work. I believed in the future we'd have—the three of us. I'd rub my belly every night, imagining what life would look like, holding on to that hope.

When the early labor came, it hit me harder than I expected. Pain, exhaustion—every moment blurred together. The sterile scent of the hospital, the blinding lights, and a fear I couldn't escape. I tried to reach Nick, but there was no answer. The nurses were kind, but their reassurances felt hollow. I wanted Nick. I needed Nick. But I was alone.

Each complication that arose felt like another blow, like I was losing control of everything. The hours dragged on, stretching into what felt like an eternity. And then, finally, our daughter arrived. They placed her in my arms for only a moment—her weight, so small and fragile, etched into my memory forever. I barely had time to see her tiny face before they whisked her away to the NICU. The room felt empty without her, without anyone. It was just me, left with the ache of what had just happened and the fear of what was still to come.

A nurse came back to help me clean up, my body torn apart, my mind racing with a thousand questions I didn't have the strength to ask. The room felt empty, and I felt smaller than ever, my thoughts a jumble of fear and uncertainty. Three hours passed. Just three hours after she was born, Nick walked back into the room. His face was pale, his eyes clouded with something I'd never seen before—fear, maybe, or something worse.

That's when the nurse spoke. Her voice was gentle, but her words cut through me like a knife. I can still hear them, echoing in my mind, even after all these years.

"I'm sorry, but your baby girl didn't make it. You can see her now."

The world stopped. The steady beeping of the machines, the low hum of the hospital, it all faded into nothingness. My heart shattered like a windscreen smashed into a million tiny shards. I remember lying there, unable to move, unable to breathe. I left the hospital without her. No baby in my arms, just a tiny picture and a card with her footprint stamped on it.

The picture is gone, and the card... I don't know where it ended up. But her footprint, the curve of it, the way it looked so perfect and small, that's etched into my heart forever.

We tried to be teenagers again, clinging to each other as we planned for college, hoping for a better future. But Nick and I were never the same after that. He was broken, so shattered by grief that I couldn't put him back together. I could barely hold myself together. Our world was crumbling, piece by piece. One night, in the middle of his grief, he came to me. His touch wasn't gentle—it felt desperate, like he was reaching for something to hold on to. But even in his arms, I felt utterly alone. There was a hollow space between us that no amount of closeness could fill.

Two months later, I was pregnant again. So fast. So fertile. It felt like the universe was trying to give us a second chance, but life isn't that simple. Nothing was. I did everything I could to protect the new life growing inside me. Everything. But Nick... Nick turned cruel. His grief had twisted into something darker—anger, resentment.

"You gonna kill this one too?" he spat, his words slicing through me, leaving a wound I knew would never heal.

Those words are still branded in my mind, cutting through me even now. How do you forget something like that? You don't. I distanced myself from him after those words, pulling away. Creating a wall between us. My focus was on the baby. Not him. Never him. I knew I wasn't making him happy, but I didn't care. My priorities had shifted.

Could he have had someone else on the side? Someone to satisfy him while I was lost in my grief?

Absolutely. He needed something I couldn't give him. Maybe that's what drove him away in the end. I used to tell myself he chose baseball over fatherhood. I told myself he couldn't handle being a dad. But maybe… maybe it's just a lie I've told myself to make it easier to forget how broken we both were.

***

I'm sitting in the car, keys in the ignition, staring at Drew's last message. I've paused my responses, unsure of what to say next. Maybe this is a philosophical conversation better suited for in person. But Drew, true to form, keeps going. I open his latest text.

> **How lucky is that guy to find someone to hook up anytime he wants!**

A laugh escapes me. Half in disbelief, half in nervousness. I send back a laughing emoji, but it feels empty. It's like we're dancing around something bigger, something I'm hesitant to name. Part of me wonders if that's what I need, too. No strings, no commitment, just... relief. The thought of opening my heart and fully committing to Drew constricts my chest. I can't go down that road again. What if he leaves, just like Nick did? What if I'm left with nothing but regret?

Pulling into the bookstore parking lot, I gather my things and fumble with my keys, the strap of my bag snagging on my sweater. Great. Awkwardness and frustration hit me all at once. *What the hell is wrong with me today?*

I dump everything behind the counter, glancing at my phone as it buzzes again. Do I even want to respond? Do I want to keep this going? Before I can decide, another text pops up.

> **You want to be my lady in the city?**

My stomach flips, and I almost drop my phone. Is he serious? Is this a joke? I'm frozen at the counter, looking at the words, rereading them to see if I can understand the hidden meaning. I must be overthinking this. *He has to be joking.*

Ha! Aren't you a funny man today?

The laughing emoji he sends back makes me roll my eyes. I push down the weird mix of nerves and excitement bubbling up inside me.

I'm at the bookstore. Time to get back to reality.

This work will not do itself lol.

Have a great day. Talk soon.

I stare at the screen, uncertain how to interpret the conversation. *Things get misconstrued over text, right?* Maybe he was just playing around. He needs to get back to the real world. And so, do I.

I glance at the towering pile of books needing to be re-shelved. It feels endless, but at least it's a distraction. I try to focus on the task at hand, pushing thoughts of Drew out of my mind. For now.

Hours pass, and thankfully, customers trickle in, giving me moments of reprieve from my wandering thoughts. Mrs. Mahone arrives at ten o'clock, asking me to fill out a book order form for August. I nod, but my mind is somewhere else entirely. I've been staring at the same page for the past twenty minutes, barely making a dent. *Just pick something.* I hope she doesn't notice how distracted I am.

By the time I finally check the clock, it's almost half past ten, and Drew is still lingering in my head. Maybe he'll bring me a coffee. I sit behind the counter, determined to refocus on the book order. But the questions keep circling back.

Does he want to be more than friends? Or maybe... maybe he just wants something easy, something simple. *Friends with benefits.* Would that be so bad? Maybe it's exactly what I need—something without strings, without the risk of heartbreak. And I wouldn't have to involve Troy. *It could work.*

But a part of me can't shake the feeling that I'm on the edge of something dangerous. A line that, once crossed, can't be undone. *Is this what I want?* My heart says one thing, but my body... my body pulls me in a different direction. Enough of this. I'm done overthinking it.

My fingers hover over the screen, and before I can talk myself out of it, my thumbs on the letters to form the words. *Fuck it.* Enough of this. I'm taking charge.

I need to see you… NOW!

Yes! Tell him what we want.

I barely register the lie spilling from my lips as I rush past Mrs. Mahone, telling her there's an emergency with Troy. Guilt flickers through me, but it's quickly snuffed out by the pressure building inside me, the urgency to see Drew. She waves me off. Her understanding about Troy stuff is always a relief, but it doesn't stop the sinking feeling I'm leaving more behind than just today's wages. Still, none of it can override the pounding need pushing me toward him.

Tell her you're a dirty girl and need to see if your friend wants to ravish you. I grip my phone tighter, my fingers trembling slightly as I type.

> **Can you meet me at the park? The one at the end of Harbour Street?**

> **Yes, I'm not far. I can be there in ten minutes. Everything okay?**

> **Yes, I need to talk to you about something. See you in ten.**

My heart races as I pull into the park just three minutes later, gravel crunching under my tires. I park and jump out, pacing near my car, the cool breeze doing nothing to calm the heat under my skin. I run the conversation through my head a thousand times, each version sounding worse than the last. *What if he doesn't want this?* My breath catches. *What if he wants more than I can give?* The thought is sharp, but I push it away.

It doesn't matter what he wants; it's what I want. Take it or leave it. *Time to take control.*

I force myself to stop pacing and click the button to lock my car, the familiar *beep beep* grounds me for just a second. My bag with my phone is safely stashed inside, and I jiggle my keys in my hand, the steady rhythm somehow helping me keep my thoughts in check. I scan the park, finding a spot near a tree with a bench. It's private enough, with only a family playing in the distance at the playground, far enough not to notice anything.

The wind tugs at my sweater, and I wrap it tighter around me. Not for warmth but for comfort, as if it can shield me from the whirlwind in my mind. My heart hammers in my chest, every beat syncing with the sound of his truck approaching. I glance up as he parks, my pulse quickening when I see him step out, tugging off his ball cap to smooth his hair before putting it back on. He's due for a haircut, but somehow, the unruly look suits him. *Focus, Charley. Focus.*

I stand, pacing in front of the bench again, my hands clenching and unclenching the edge of my sweater. I feel the tension crackling in the air between us as he walks toward me, his eyes locked on mine. Each step feels like an eternity, and my mind races faster with every passing second.

This is it. No turning back.

He motions a hello as he approaches and takes a seat on the bench. "You want to sit?"

"I can't, yet," I answer.

He leans back on the bench, casually stretching an arm across the backrest like he's got all the time in the world. The smoothness of the gesture makes my own movements feel jerky and awkward in comparison. I clutch the keys in my hand, trying to still the nervous jiggling, but the urge to fidget is overwhelming. I take a deep breath, the cool air filling my lungs, and steel myself just to say it.

His brow furrows as he studies me, his voice low and filled with concern. "Charley, are you okay? Is Troy okay? What's wrong?"

I swallow, feeling the lump in my throat. "Troy is fine. Nothing's wrong with him. It's just… " I pause, the words clinging to the back of my throat. My heart hammers in my chest. "Something's on my mind, and it couldn't wait. We need to talk."

The breeze rustles the leaves overhead, but all I can focus on is the heavy silence hanging between us, waiting for me to break it.

"That's not usually a good thing," he says, shifting his elbows to his knees to lean forward. The sleeves of his plain black golf shirt stretch tight around his biceps. Damn him with those arms!

"Is this about my text? You know, I was just playing around. I'm sorry if you... " His words tumble out quickly, but I raise my hand to stop him mid-sentence.

"Please, let me speak." My voice is firmer than I expect, but inside, I feel my pulse racing, my nerves jumping.

His mouth snaps shut, his jaw tightening, and I see the flicker of regret in his eyes as he presses his lips into a thin line, like he's holding back more words. The tension in the air is almost suffocating, but I know I have to push through it.

"I love our friendship," I begin, my voice softer now. "And I don't want to ruin anything by not being very direct with you about how I'm feeling... or what I'm thinking."

My chest tightens as I force myself to keep going, to lay it all out there. The weight of the moment is pressing down on me, but I take a deep breath, trying to steady myself.

His eyes soften, and he cuts in, "I'm so sorry, Charley. I shouldn't have texted what I did."

I cut him off again, my hand lifting slightly to stop the apology I know is coming. The breeze tugs at my sweater, and I pull it closer, seeking comfort as the weight of what I'm about to say presses down on me.

"You have to let me get this out," I say, my voice steady but tight.

He nods, his pupils dilated, and I can tell he's bracing for something, but I'm not sure if he's prepared for what comes next.

The seriousness in my tone seems to shift the air between us, thick with anticipation. I rewrap the edges of my sweater tighter around myself, trying to steady the trembling inside. For a moment, I close my eyes, pulling together whatever courage I have left.

When I open them, Drew is still sitting there, watching me, his expression softer now.

It hits me how vulnerable we both are in this moment, and all I want to do is reach out, to touch him, to reassure him that this isn't about pulling away but getting closer to something real.

He stands and starts walking toward me, his eyes locked on mine. My heart skips. *Is he going to hug me?*

Panic flutters in my chest, and before I can think, the words rush out. "I don't want something serious or out in the open," I blurt, my hand shooting up to stop him from coming any closer. The movement feels instinctive, like I need to create space before this moment swallows me whole.

His steps falter, and the warmth in his eyes shifts, flickering between confusion and understanding as he freezes just a few feet away. The air between us hums with something unspoken, and I feel the weight of my words settling into the silence.

"And I don't want Troy to know. So, can we keep this a secret?" I ask.

He nods in agreement, mouth gaping a little. *I think we took his ability to speak.*

"I want a friends-with-benefits kind of arrangement, just sex. I don't want to date you. I still want my friend and do all the other things we've always done." I watch for his reaction or interruption, but he just keeps staring at me, unsure how to digest this information.

"If after the first time, we think this isn't for us, then we stop. Friendship comes first. Agreed?" I ask.

I want to keep talking, but I know if I keep rambling, I'm going to want to touch him, and my boundary will be all for nothing. *Stay strong.*

He doesn't speak; he looks away at the family near the playground, who now seem to be packing up to head out. Taking a long breath and removing his ball cap, he flexes the brim in his hands. *He does that when he needs a moment to think.* He looks at me and smiles.

"Yeah, I would be okay with that," and puts the hat on backwards.

My knees nearly buckle. *Jump into his arms and tell him to take you right here on the bench.* I don't think he realizes the little ball cap move is my kryptonite. The way he casually adjusts it, smoothing his hair before settling it back in place. It's such a simple gesture, but it stirs something deep inside me. How does something so effortless make me want him so badly? His confident, boyish charm pulls me in, unraveling any sense of control I thought I had.

My body hums with need, my thoughts dark and reckless. A part of me wants to sink to my knees right here and tell him exactly what I want. *Claim my mouth, let me feel him completely.* It's taking all my self-control to keep my hands to myself and my legs firmly planted. I swallow the saliva gathering in my mouth. "Great, okay, that's it then," I say as I fiddle with my keys. I don't want to look away from him. Not yet. I feel trapped in this moment. I don't know what to do.

"We will talk more later?" he says as he comes toward me, arms outstretched.

"Stop! Please," I say. Using my hand to fill the space between us again. We've hugged a few times before, but this time feels different. I'm worried he might misunderstand my abrupt gesture.

"You can't touch me, please. Not today." I don't know how else to articulate the way my body would betray me if he put his hands on me now.

"Okay," he says.

I nod and start walking toward my car.

He follows without a word.

I point my keys at my car to open the door.

"Talk soon?" he asks, waiting for me to get inside.

"Always," I say as I put my car in reverse and head home.

After seeing Drew, I'm on autopilot, sitting in my car in the garage at quarter after eleven on a Wednesday.

What do I do now? I'm sure Margaret will wonder why I'm home early as I head into the house. I kick off my shoes and dump my bag at the door, realizing how much I need to sit down to process what just happened.

As I enter the living room, I see the sun pouring into the space. I'm rarely home this time of day, so I forget how amazing it looks. So calm and inviting. As I plop into my reading chair, I'm grateful to have a few moments of peace. As the sun shines down on me, its radiant golden light fills me with a sense of warmth and comfort.

I curl up my leg in a gentle, protective hug. I let myself fully embrace the calm. *I did it.* I wrap my protective sweater tightly around me, allowing my thoughts to flow freely.

I did what I wanted, and I said what I wanted. "It was the right thing," I mutter to myself, determined this will not change our friendship or blow up my life. We are adults, and we can figure this out. *Now, let's have some fun.*

12

IT COULDN'T WAIT

DREW

I'm speechless... relieved... stunned. What just happened? Watching her hold her sweater around herself was agonizing. It was like if she let go, she would come apart at the seams, and I didn't know what to do. I didn't know what she wanted me to do.

When she texted, I thought something had happened. Then, as I watched her pace, I was expecting her to give me heck about the 'lady in the city' text. Yell, scream, tell me I'm an asshole for making such a stupid comment. My intention was to be playful, it backfired, and all morning, I was trying to figure out how to smooth it over.

I never expected it to go like that. Wow, she is full of surprises. *It's why she's so intriguing.*

I feel my phone vibrate in my pocket, and I quickly open it, hoping it's Charley. I sigh when I see it's a message from Britt.

> Change of plans. You will have to come and get your stuff on Friday. Saturday won't work.

I take a deep breath and run through my mental agenda. Gran moved to another unit, and she isn't coming home soon. They want her to get stronger before she is discharged. Each time we review her gains, and I tease her she will bulk up soon enough.

> Friday will be fine. I will be there by noon. I'll head out before sunrise.

> Do you want me to text you when I'm leaving?

Yes, that will work. Thanks for understanding, Drew.

Friday is not a big deal. My days are the same every day, and it's about time I get my stuff out of that apartment. Time to start a new life.

***

My trip to Denver went better than I expected. Charley says she is busy at the bookstore, so we've only had a few quick chats and updates. No mention of our new arrangement, except we agreed not to force it.

"It will happen when it happens," she says.

Although I agree, I can't help but wonder when.

It's now Monday. The weekend went by in a blur. Gran had a bit of a setback yesterday and she's now back on the medical unit because she has a lung infection that requires intravenous antibiotics every eight hours. The medicine makes her feel dizzy, and she now wears a bracelet with HIGH FALL RISK in red letters. Aunt Christine stays with her most of the time now. This morning, she told me she is 'fine', but I know there's hidden meaning in the word. I'm just not sure what the meaning is yet.

It's almost half past ten. Charley likely needs a caffeine fix. As I pull the door of the bookstore open, balancing two coffees, her face lights up as she comes to greet me.

"Perfect timing," she says as she takes the cup from my hand and leads us to one of the sitting areas off to the side. "I've had quite the morning, and I need a break."

Hearing her voice as she tells her story fills me with a calmness I didn't know I needed. I sit back and enjoy her animated gestures.

"They were yelling at each other! Yelling, 'I found it first!' Can you imagine? Two people fighting over a Christoph?"

"I can't imagine," I say, smiling. I'm sure she knows I don't know what a Christoph is, I'm not sure I want to know, but this isn't about me. It's about how adorable she looks as she tells her story and pauses to sip her coffee.

Half of my coffee is gone. I need it hot, and so I enjoyed the first sips before I got here. It's lukewarm in my hands now; no rush to finish it.

She looks at her phone to check the time. "I should get back. Thanks so much for the coffee."

I stand with her, and we are inches apart. I want to hug her. *Should I ask?* I haven't touched her since we spoke that day in the park. I'm not sure where we stand on the whole touching thing now, so I hesitate, not wanting to overstep. There's something about her that makes me want to get it right, to let her set the pace.

Instead, I watch her and try to read her body language, hoping for some kind of signal. She just stands there, waiting. Neither of us moving, like we're caught in the tension of what could happen next.

Follow her lead, I remind myself, unsure of whether to close the gap between us or keep my distance.

"You okay?" I ask.

Her breathing speeds up, hands holding the coffee in front of her chest. "Yes, I guess..." She sits back down, her voice soft. "I just got a little dizzy."

"Give me this." I gently take her coffee before she spills it. "Sit back, it's okay. I'm right here. It'll pass."

She leans into the chair, and I can see her tension ease a bit. "My brain was going a mile a minute. Maybe I shouldn't have any more caffeine," she says with a small laugh.

"No more coffee... today," I tease, and she chuckles. The sound is like a wave of relief washing over me; her smile warms the space between us.

"I know we said we'd let things happen organically, but..." I pause, the words lingering on my lips. "I want to scoop you up in my arms right now and take you home."

Her hand reaches for mine but stops midway, hesitating as if the world might be watching. "It'll happen when it's supposed to happen," she says softly, adjusting her glasses, her eyes darting away. I wonder if she's just as nervous about all of this as I am, the weight of the moment tugging at us both.

I harden at the thought of kissing her. I glance around and it seems no one is in the store now, a relief that I don't have to worry someone will overhear our conversation.

"You are working alone today?" I ask.

"Only this morning, Mrs. Mahone is coming in after lunch. She wants to see how I've set up the new display," she says. As she speaks, she runs her fingers through her hair and twists the strands to one side. Witnessing this nervous habit makes my heart speed up. It's so Charley.

"Feeling better?" I say.

"Yes, much better. Thank you," she says as she bites her lower lip, making it hard to restrain myself. Is it too soon to kiss her? Is this considered too public? *I can't just jump on her like an animal.*

"You are heading out to get Gran some cupcakes?" she asks.

"You remember my routine?" I say.

"Hard to forget. We first bumped into each other when you got them the first time, remember?"

"Yes, how could I forget?" My world hums, everything sharpening as her face lights up at the memory. She's talking, but her words are fading, drowned out by the way her mouth moves, the soft curve of her lips as they shape each sound. I can't stand it any longer.

I stand abruptly, and she stops mid-sentence, confusion flickering in her eyes. But before she can say anything, I grip the armrests of her chair and lean in, my body drawn to hers as if I've been waiting for this moment forever. I don't hesitate. I press my lips to hers and taste the warmth of her, unable to control the overwhelming urge any longer.

Her body tenses for a second, a flicker of surprise, but then I feel it, the soft surrender in the way she exhales. The tension melts away. My hand tightens on the armrest as if to hold on to the moment, hoping like hell this doesn't change everything between us. But when a soft sigh slips from her lips, I know it's too late. Everything is already changing.

There it is... surrender.

I pull back, but her head follows mine. A last, desperate attempt to keep the connection alive. Her lips are sweet and so goddamn perfect I can't help but wonder why the hell I waited so long.

"I couldn't wait anymore," I murmur, still hovering above her, heart pounding. Her eyes meet mine, and I feel it deep in my gut.

It's time to take what I want.

13

THE LETTING GO

CHARLEY

I am home getting ready to head to Drew's. After our time at the bookstore today, we made plans to see each other tonight. I've checked on Margaret, and she is all set up for the evening with her shows. Our chat yesterday after church went well, so today was a quick check in with my Monday check of making sure Miss Camilla's litter was clean.

The video game sounds from Troy's room reassure me, he is distracted while I get ready. My plan is to tell him I need to check something at the store and not to wait up. That's happened a few times before, so I don't suspect he will get suspicious or ask questions. *Not like you can tell him what you are really doing.*

Drew is expecting me in an hour; I'm just not sure how to get ready for the possibility of it being our first time having sex. After our first kiss, he left with a "We need to do more of that" comment. *We need a lot more than that!*

I don't want to assume he will want to have me tonight, but no harm in being prepared. I jump in the shower and wash up. Thinking about our kiss, I let the warm water soothe me. His lips touching mine felt familiar. Allowing myself to dissolve into the memory. I don't know what I thought it would be like, but I didn't expect his lips on mine to leave me breathless and momentarily freeze my world. I've read about it in books. I didn't think it was real!

I step out of the shower and look at myself in the mirror. I wonder if I should put on make-up and what to wear. *Maybe a dress?*

Remembering I'm supposed to be heading to the bookstore, a dress is out of the question. I put on yoga pants and a T-shirt, my evening uniform.

This is definitely a benefit of our arrangement. Comfortable clothes, no make-up or weird dating conversation. I look at my phone and realize the time.

I hadn't been to Martha's before, but I knew what neighbourhood she was in when Drew texted me her address. I approach the door, and my nerves kick in. Am I really doing this? My heart wants to leap out of my chest as I give a quiet three-tap knock and slowly open the door.

"In here," he calls from another room, and I follow his voice. As I round the corner, he is getting up off the couch.

"Hi," I say, noticing his evening attire is the same as what he wore earlier: jeans and a dark grey t-shirt, the fabric stretching across his shoulders, making it look like it's one size too small. *Is it something he does on purpose, or does he just need new clothes?*

He abruptly stops as he sees me standing six feet away, pausing ever so subtly and breathing out a quiet 'hh-hi.' His awkwardness is so unfamiliar, it makes me smile. He moves toward me, and I ask a question but can't get out the words before his mouth crashes into mine.

Grabbing the back of my head, fingers moving through my hair, I melt into him as his lips part, and his tongue sweeps into my mouth. My arms wrap around his shoulders and lean into him with more need than intended. I have no self-control. *I need more.*

I feel the magnet-like pull towards him as my knees weaken. He puts his other arm lower on my back to hold me close and moves my hair to the side to expose my neck to nip at my skin. My doubts disappear. My vulnerability exposed. *Let go!*

If this was going to be our only time, I shouldn't hold back. I don't want to hold back. I need a release. He stops kissing my neck and I feel the absence of him immediately. *I guess he shouldn't take me in the hallway.* He leads me by the hand into the living room, and I notice the neatness of the room. The one side has shelves of collectibles, reminding me we are in Martha's home. The curtains are drawn, but they don't quite meet in the middle. I hope the neighbours are not too curious.

My thoughts about my surroundings vanish as he kisses me again and lifts my shirt to sweep it up over my head. I stand in my bra and yoga pants.

"Beautiful. I've wanted to see those for so long," he says before diving into my breasts, cupping them and pulling down my bra to expose me. As he licks my hardened nipples, I watch his delight, but I am feeling lightheaded, feeling the string down my center to my core being tugged. *How is he doing that?*

I open my chest, giving myself over to him. Seeming so new, yet familiar. I reach down to touch him, feeling the length of him in jeans. I want him so badly. *Oh, please be a nice one!*

He stops indulging as if he can hear my inner dirty girl needing to find out what is inside those jeans. He opens his belt, which feels like it takes forever. I want to say something flirty, but I'm at a loss for words.

Is he as nervous as I am? I drop to my knees and help him. His eyes go wide, not expecting me to be so bold. Helping him take off his pants, springing him out to greet me.

"Well, hello, nice to meet you," I say. *That's a welcome surprise.*

He laughs as he uses his feet to step out of his jeans and socks. "I am trying not to be too eager, but you are making this impossible," he says.

"Good. You took off your socks," I smirk as I get on my knees in front of him.

"No socks. Damn Charley," he says as I pull my hair back and raise my hand to take off my glasses. "No, please leave those on. Just for a moment?" he asks as I look up at him and wait to see if he will let me taste.

"As you wish," I say, hands outstretched. Even though it's hard for me to see him clearly with my glasses on when he is this close, I can't miss the way he twitches in anticipation. My hand moves to touch his hip, and he lets me decide the next move. *I want this. I need this.*

I hope he understands how much the dirty girl inside me needs to be let out. His hand cups my face, the warmth of his palm grounding me as his thumb gently brushes my cheek. I feel the heat of his touch sinking into my skin, and instinctively, I place my hands on my thighs, waiting. Waiting for him to make the next move, to close the distance between us again. My pulse quickens, and the air between us feels electric, heavy with the unspoken.

"I love you in glasses," he says, and I smile at the way he can make something so ordinary sound special. I'm impressed by the way he controls himself with my lips, only inches from his tip.

"Can I?" I say as I open my mouth wide and flatten my tongue out to receive him. I close my eyes in anticipation that he will move forward.

"Well, aren't you exactly what I need?" he says as he bends down and kisses my forehead. "Take what you want, Charley, let me see." *Permission.* He is giving me permission.

My insides purr with pleasure as I take him in my hand and guide the tip into my mouth. My nostrils are filled with his scent as I inhale him. I've smelled that musk on him before, after he's had a workout. His salty taste has a bit of soap mixed in, likely left from his shower.

His length slides deeper into my mouth, and he takes in a breath as he puts his hand in my hair.

"Damn," he breathes down at me. His response to my mouth helps me focus on my task.

No thoughts to interrupt my pleasure enter my mind. It has been so long since I have done this, and I realize how much I've missed it. *The control.* My pleasure of taking what I want. My mind switches to thoughts of how I could make this better for him, for me. The balance of staying in the moment and floating away with pleasure. I rock back and forth between these two states until I give over to my inner dirty girl. *Time to come out and play.*

He gets harder in my mouth just when I didn't think it was possible. I circled the tip with my tongue, tasting the sweetness. I pop my lips off his tip and smile.

"Where did you learn that?" He breathes as he takes me by the shoulders to help me stand.

I don't answer since no answer is best.

He growls, "My turn."

Before I can process his words, he throws me over his shoulder and heads down a hallway.

"What are you doing?" I laugh as he slaps my ass. I can see his powerful legs beneath the hem of his t-shirt as he strides, each step confident and strong.

"Change of scenery," he says as we enter a bedroom. He puts me down and takes off his shirt. He is standing naked in front of me, his erection emphasizing my target.

"This used to be a sitting room, but I've claimed it as my new room since the one upstairs is small. You like it?" he asks.

My head is nodding to show I understand, but my thoughts are scattered. Gently, he lifts my chin, guiding my eyes to meet his, bringing me back to the moment.

My mouth can't seem to form words, so I nod again as I let his hands wander around my body. He pops off my bra, cupping my breast with both hands, kissing and sucking. Was that a little bite?

He guides my pants to the floor, and before I can figure out what he might do next, my panties are gone with them. He is crouched, kissing my stomach. My knees weaken at the sight of his head and the strength of his hands on my body.

"Lie down," he commands, coming up for air.

I obey, trying to follow his hands and mouth, that seem to cover me in all the neglected spots, making me moan.

"Oh god," I breathe. This is nothing like I've ever experienced before, or is it just because it's been so long?

His mouth between my legs finds my clit with ease, and for what feels like seconds, I ride the wave. "Oh, God!" I say.

His fingers find their way inside until I arch and scream his name. *I'm flying.* My orgasm comes so fast. Is it over already? I don't want it to end. *Don't open your eyes.*

I know he isn't done, but how do I follow that?

"Well, that was unexpected," I say as he smiles at my splayed body on his bed.

"You need a break? Food? Water?" he asks.

"I'm good," I breathe. I don't want to move, but I'm good. *I am more than good.*

He kisses me softly, and I roll toward him. "Where did you learn that?" His head tilts back in a laugh. We lay, and I breathe in the last moments of my release. *Amazing.*

"No one has seemed to enjoy it as much as you just did," he says.

"Really? Well, that is interesting. What other talents might you have, Mr. Stanton, sir?" I ask. My playful side makes him laugh again, and I can't help but roll him over and straddle him. "Ready for the next round?"

"Oh, I think I'm going to like this side of you, Miss Thomas," he says as I lean down to kiss him. He pulls me closer, my breasts pressing against his chest. My body aches for more. If we get this out of our system, maybe we can go back to just being friends. *Liar. Naïve. As if that's the last time, I want to experience Mr. Andrew Michael Stanton.*

DREW

Charley can let go! I've never had a woman who did that with me before. Certainly not Britt. She was fun and liked to try a lot of things but couldn't let herself enjoy the orgasm ride.

Witnessing Charley's orgasm with my tongue and fingers, I have a feeling Britt was faking it. Although she would never admit that to me.

Charley takes me by surprise as she rolls on top of me. Not the shy or reserved woman she presents in public. I knew her *dirty girl* was lingering below the surface. She just needed a little coaxing to come out.

"Ride me," I command to see if the fire in her eyes will flicker again. I want to be inside her so badly; to claim this sexual goddess. Her moans escape her throat as she lets me slide inside.

"So tight," I say.

"You feel so good," she says between breaths as she rocks up and down. Her expressions make my job easier; no need to guess what she enjoys. She doesn't hold in her moans, which spurred me to want more.

I need more. I grab her torso to get her to stop. "My turn," I say. I flip her on her back and hold her legs open with my hands, testing how much I can stretch her hips. I realize Britt would have asked me to stop, saying I was too rough. *Stop comparing the two!*

If women have a combination lock, I've always felt confused trying to figure out the code. *Not Charley.* Unlocking her was such a simple task. No games. I feel like she handed me the code, and now it leaves me curious. *I want more.*

My mind clears of comparisons as I watch how Charley's body responds as I thrust inside her, confident she can take all of me. I pull her to the edge of the bed, trying to be gentle, but I can't slow down. The ache inside of me needs release and will not wait. Her back arches, and she puts her hands above her head to grab the blankets as I hold her legs while they shake. An orgasm takes over her body, and we hold on until it subsides.

Her eyes don't find mine to reassure me, but as the moans and rapid breathing slow, her body tells me everything I need to know. Did I unlock a deeper part of her that needed to be free? I need to see it again. Feel it again. Feel her again.

And again, and again.

14

THE INVITATION

CHARLEY

Two weeks have passed, and Drew and I are still figuring out our new dynamic. Our routine was disrupted a little with the new arrangements for Martha, but I'm happy I still get to see him almost every day.

I keep looking out the window, hoping he will arrive with coffee soon. I blame the end of school and the start of summer holidays, affecting the slow traffic in the store and a drop in sales. Mrs. Mahone left to see her mother again, so my store duties were done within the first thirty minutes.

"Oh, thank god! There you are." I pop from my seat to grab the coffee.

"Hard day?" he says.

"Funny man, you know I'm bored out of my tree! Tell me how Gran is doing. Did you get her all settled?" My desperation for conversation doesn't seem to put him off as he flops into the chair beside me and puts a bag on the floor beside him.

"She is all settled at Aunt Christine's, and I think she is already tired of the fussing. I feel bad that I couldn't help her move back home. She's thinking she'll sell the house now. Her strength isn't what it used to be, and it's just too much to think about how she will be independent in a two-story house."

"I'm so sorry Drew. When do you think it will happen?" I ask.

"Not for a few weeks. She agreed to let things settle. The room is set up as best as possible. I know she gets upset at my aunt sometimes, but deep down, I know she is relieved to be out of the hospital," he says.

"It feels like she has been there too long," I add.

"Absolutely. I admit, I won't miss that place," he says, handing me the bag beside him. "Here are the books she borrowed. She didn't give me another list. I'll let her settle first."

"Thank you," I say with a little sadness in my heart as I take it from him. "I'll be ready when she gives me a new list."

"Thank you," he sighs and lays his head back in the chair. "I could go for a nap," he says as he closes his eyes, but I am exploding with excitement.

"Well, I have news... want to know now or later?" I say.

"Now!"

"Well, that woke you up!" I say.

"Is it fun news?" he asks.

"You will never guess," I tease.

"I know, but I like to guess."

"Oh, I know, but even if we do twenty questions, you won't get it."

"Fine, tell me. Spoilsport." He waves me away.

"Ha! You might not think that in a moment," I say as he puts his elbows on his knees, and I mirror his movements. "I got a call from my friend Tina; you remember her from high school?"

"Ya... "

"Well, she moved to Ridgeport a while back for a job, and she just got promoted again. She is moving to Texas!"

"I'm happy for her, but it's not the fun news I was expecting."

"I know, I know. I'm not done," I say as his hands gesture for me to keep going. "She is throwing a weekend bash on Lake Wiokka, and she invited everyone to go. She called me and told me to tell you. Now, before you start in with all the questions, I just thought we might go for a bit on the Saturday. I checked and Troy doesn't have a game that day. We can park down the road so no one will know we came together, but I think going to this will be good for us. Lots of fun and... we can hide in plain sight."

"She's just having a big party for herself?" his mind processing the information.

"Yes, and we can go. Have some fun. Maybe we can remember we are only thirty-five? Maybe forget we are a mom and a grandson for an afternoon? What do you think?" I ask.

"I'm thirty-six," he says, smirking.

"Fine. Thirty-six. You ole man, you." I say.

"Free food?" he asks.

"Yes, but maybe we should bring something? Best to not show up empty-handed." I lean back in the chair, waiting for more of his questions.

"Well, if we have to bring something, I don't want to go now," he smirks.

"Of course you do." I hear the chime from the front door, signaling I have a customer.

"You think Shawn from biology class will be there?" he asks as I approach one of my regular customers, hoping to make a sale today.

I turn back toward Drew and notice he is relaxed in the chair, enjoying the last of his coffee. "Oh, I wonder if he still has the mullet!" I say as he laughs and puts his head back on the chair, closing his eyes. I know he has been under so much stress lately; I wonder what is in store for him next. The party will be an excellent distraction for him. *For us.*

$$\infty$$

15

TINA'S PARTY

CHARLEY

The drive to Tina's party was filled with predictions of how people would have changed since 1996. "I should have brought my yearbook," I say, making the last turn toward Lake Wiokka.

"You still have it?" Drew asked.

"You don't? I'm shocked," I say, putting my hand on my heart.

"I'm sure Gran has it on a shelf somewhere." He waves his hand in dismissal of my mocking gesture.

The GPS tells us we are within two hundred feet of our destination. "I'm going to park here. You okay to walk? I don't want it to be obvious we came together."

"Sure," he says as I pull behind a black SUV. I insisted we take my car today since his truck was full of things to donate from Martha's house.

"We're sticking to the plan?" he confirms, his hand on the car door handle, ready to jump out.

"Yes. I definitely want to be back before dark. No need to worry Margaret," I say hoping my sarcastic tone is clear. Ever since the Michael set up didn't go as she planned, she seems very intent on knowing all about my social life. I keep telling her I don't need a matchmaker, but something about my refusal has spurred her into action. *But why?*

As we walk toward the party house, it's obvious where we're going. Cars are parked on both sides of the road and *Dancing Queen* blares out from the speakers as we near the lane. It's easy to join the crowd. No one notices we came together.

Drew winks at me and mouths, "Have fun."

I smile back, watching him head toward the front yard; I head into the house, looking for Tina.

The hours slip by as I listen to stories and reminisce about our high school years. Most of them have young kids now and are using this party to escape from parental duties; the alcohol flows, and the voices grow louder. I nurse my second vodka soda, knowing if I have any more, I will need a nap.

From my stolen glances at Drew, I spot he has a beer can in his hand. I don't recognize the label, and I haven't seen him take it to his lips once.

He catches my eye, and I gesture a *cheers* in his direction. He mirrors my action but looks down at the can and rolls his eyes with a yuck notion.

I laugh and quickly cover my mouth with my free hand, so no one notices our silent conversation. I'm enjoying being close without being close and try not to smile, thinking of how someone across the room has been secretly bending me over for a few weeks. Blushing, I turn away so he can't see the thoughts flickering across my face, memories of our last time in his truck at the park. Like two teenagers who can't get enough. *Yes, bend me over, please.*

I am slightly entertained as I stand on the edge of the conversation circle while Tina tells about her adventures. She loves the attention, and I'm happy to give some of mine to her. The rest of it is for Drew, hoping he doesn't notice how I keep watching him out of the corner of my eye. Well, not really him. It's more what the blonde bombshell is doing beside him. I think it's Joanne, but I can't remember for sure.

All I know is the way she strokes his arm is making me agitated. *It shouldn't matter, we aren't a couple.* She twirls her hair as she hangs on his every word. Oh god, is that what women do? Do men like that? No wonder my dates have gone so badly.

"Oh, stop it," I hear Joanne say to Drew. Her flirty hand lands on his chest and lingers a second too long. *What was that?* Drew catches my eye, and I look away, trying to pretend I've not been watching them.

I turn to take some chips from the communal bowl, trying not to think about who else has had their hands in it. I taste a soggy chip and want to spit them all out. *Oh gawd, where is the washroom? This is so gross.* I cough and cover my mouth, hoping not to draw any attention to myself. *So ladylike.*

"Down the wrong hatch?" I hear someone say beside me. I nod politely, wanting to excuse myself for a moment. *I don't recognise their face. God, why can't I remember names?*

I glance at Drew, who points at something for Joanne to look at as he mouths to me, *let's go.* The desperate rescue we both need. You don't have to tell me twice. I look at Tina. She won't notice my absence. I make friendly nods to people as I pass, hoping they don't realize I'm bailing. I don't need anyone grabbing me and saying, "Don't leave! You can't leave yet. It's not even four o'clock." *Yes, we can! Drew said it's time to go, and we are going to him. NOW.*

I meet him on the road, and we don't talk until we get into the car. "Well, that was fun," I say, starting my car and putting it into drive.

"Loads, I'm glad to get out of there." He sighs, putting his hand on my leg. "Confession?" he says.

"Joanne gave you her number?" I guess, turning the corner, trying to ignore the glide of his hand.

"God, that was awful. No, that's not my confession," he says.

"Okay, tell me then," I say as I glance at him and see he is leaning closer to me.

"It has been extremely difficult not to touch you all afternoon," he says. Well, that wasn't what I expected. He pushes my hair from my neck and starts planting kisses. We are not even a mile down the road. *How can I focus?*

"Eyes on the road," he says as his hand slides into my t-shirt.

"What are you doing, Drew?" I ask.

His playful laugh wakes my core. "Just focus on the road," he says.

I do my best to keep my eyes on the road as he moves his hands from my breast down, stretching the waistband of my shorts.

Oh, this is going to be harder than I thought.

~∞~

16

FOREST ADVENTURE

CHARLEY

My moan only encourages him as his fingers find their way down.

"No panties? Naughty girl," he says as my body responds to the two fingers he slips inside. "Oh my, someone likes that."

My eyes flutter, trying to focus on the road. *How long have I been driving?* My concentration shifts to how his fingers work their way up and down my entrance, rubbing in little circles. I take my foot off the gas; I want to pull over.

"What's wrong? Can't do two things at once?" he teases.

I answer with a breathy *yes,* but it's no use. I need to stop. There doesn't seem to be a lot of traffic on this little winding road through the trees.

"Did I take a wrong turn?" I ask.

"No, pull over here," he says, and I put the car in park and open my legs further to let his fingers dance in the wetness. As the first wave of orgasm hits me, I lean back in my seat. *Claim those fingers!*

"There you go," he purrs. As my body relaxes, he kisses my neck and puts his fingers inside my mouth. I lick them, enjoying the taste of myself. "I like when you just go with the flow," he says.

"Wow. I guess that's been building all afternoon," I say.

"I know," he says, moving back into his seat and adjusting his shorts. I see how his length is pressing into his zipper.

"Are you okay?" I ask.

"I'll be fine. You okay to drive?"

"Of course. Thank you for taking the edge off," I say, pulling back onto the road. My driving isn't as smooth as I can't seem to keep the right speed, and my corners are off.

"Pull off at the next right," he says in a firm tone, pointing at the sign up ahead.

"Is my driving that bad?" I read the sign that says, 'No exit'.

He doesn't answer as I slow to make the turn. It seems to be a private dirt road with a few houses nestled in a bush. I wonder if there are lots for sale. It looks like a nice place to build a dream home.

"I think I'll drive," he says.

I don't hesitate, I want to give over control of this car. I am eager to get into the passenger side, but as we pass each other at the front bumper, he grabs my arm and pulls me into a kiss.

I melt into him. I do not know if anyone can see us. *I don't care.* I'm now locked into him, and my need to have this moment blocks out my surroundings. His hands roam my body, and I palm his length. *He's just as turned on by this adventure.*

He pulls off my shorts, freeing one leg, and my sandal tumbles off. I don't get to think about where it landed as he gently pushes me into the hood of the car. Like magic, I feel a protective bubble around us to explore each other.

"I need you. Take me, Drew," I beg. I pull his waistband toward me, and he shimmies them down to show me his hardness. I grab his shoulders as he lifts my legs off the ground. Shorts dangle on one thigh as the other sandal hangs between my toes.

My fear of falling is dashed away as his arms hold me with ease. I open my legs more as his tip rubs against my entrance. My body welcomes him, but the fullness makes me moan as I feel every inch of him. He holds my hips, and I link my ankles behind him as we rock against the car. *Savor this moment.*

I tilt my head, looking at the sky, bouncing slightly with our movements. *I am exactly where I'm supposed to be.*

Sounds of a car approaching halts us, and we untangle ourselves, laughing at our exposed nature. "False alarm, they are on the other road," he reassures me.

I put my shorts back on as I look for my lost sandal. It's not far, and my barefoot finds it effortlessly. I glance down and realize my shorts are twisted, sitting awkwardly on my hips. *Cute little shorts that make access less complicated.*

Maybe I should be embarrassed, but I don't care. I look at Drew and feel giddy at the naughtiness of our moment. *I need more.* He grabs my hand and pulls me to the trunk of the car. "Watch for cars," he says as he takes my shorts down to my ankles.

I position my hands, staring through the back window and down the road as he slips back inside me from behind. The slap of his hips on my ass has me losing focus, and I close my eyes to heighten the sensation. *Oh yes, take me like this! Please! Give it to me.*

I put my hands out wider on the trunk to brace myself as I hear the wetness of him gliding in and out. *I want more.*

His movements slow, and I am denied my sweet release. *No, keep going!*

"But I," I say as he pulls my shorts up and grabs my hand again.

"Come on," he says, seeing my disappointment but not giving it any attention. *He has that look in his eyes.*

He takes the keys and locks the car, never letting my hand go, so I'm pulled with every action he takes. Finally, he moves toward the treed lot on the other side of the road. I'm jerked along, not falling into step as quick as he wants.

"Come on!" he repeats, skipping towards the trees, swinging our hands between us as I catch up. Laughing, I mirror his movement like we are six years old heading to the park. *I love this playful side.*

"I want some privacy," he explains as we step over fallen trees and find a spot just down the slope of a hill.

Moments of doubt cross my mind. *Where are we? What are we doing? Are there people around? Is this private property?*

We stop by a fallen tree, and I lift my eyes to the canopy of trees. I have to squint at the sunlight that dapples down on us. *We are alone.*

"It's just us. Let me clear that head of yours," he says, taking my face in his hands and leaning in to kiss my mouth.

My body relaxes into him as my mind asks if he wants to sit me down on the log.

"Damn Charley." He breathes as I moan into his words and wrap my hands around his shoulders. His tongue finds my earlobe as I look behind him, half expecting a deer to appear. *Or maybe a rabbit.*

He navigates me closer to a tree, hands massage my ass cheeks. The sensation of him palming me helps me forget about our surroundings. *I want him inside me.*

"God, you feel so good. Lean into that tree," he says as he turns me around. Before I can overthink, I'm holding a tree, and my arms can wrap around its span so I can see into the bush. He lowers my shorts to my ankles again.

"Now that's a view," he says as he grabs me from behind and pulls my ass towards him. His hands hold me, and I bend down, feeling a slight scrape of the bark on my arms. It's worth it to have this angle. I wait, wet with anticipation that he will thrust inside me again. I need to feel his length.

Supporting my hips, he grips my cheeks, pulling it apart to get a better view.

I dip lower again, no shame in showing him my wetness and how much I need him.

"You need me inside you?" he says into my ear.

I am so turned on by the way his breath feels, a fire heats my insides. *Fill me up.*

"Take me, Drew," I say, leaning more into the tree some more than he frees himself from his pants and rubs the tip along my wetness. Teasing my entrance. The roughness of the bark through my shirt, digging into my neck, balances the pleasure pain barrier.

He is toying with me.

I want this so badly. I steady myself against the tree, the trunk stable between my neck and shoulder. Reaching behind, I grab myself to open wider for him. He thrusts inside me, letting me feel the pressure inside and the scrape of the bark. It's enough to keep my wits about me as his thrusts quicken. I rotate my hips upward to see if he could go deeper to push my boundaries.

"Fuck me, Drew!" I scream as I feel my orgasm taking over. The sound of wetness, as he slams into my center, makes my back arch and my eyes roll. *Yes! YES!*

He pulls out before I can finish. Why did he stop? I'm not finished. I move my hands back to the tree and feel his fingers rubbing all along my center. Thumb taking the wetness and circling my clit.

"Damn Charley, you are so wet." He shifts behind me, and I feel his fingers move inside me. My eyes roll again as I lose control out here with only the wildlife to see.

Let's hope there are no voyeurs nearby.

I adjust my feet, trying to open more for his hands, when I feel his hand shift and his thumb circle my other entrance.

"I want this," he says. It's barely a whisper, and I don't know if it was meant for me to hear. His thumb continues to play as he enters me, testing my reaction.

It is exhilarating.

"Oh my Gawd," I say. Nothing else exists, just the tree holding me up, the sun beaming through the leaves warming me, his fingers inside my pussy, and his thumb in my ass. My mind is numb from pleasure like I've never had before. I didn't know it could feel this good.

"I want to cum in here," he whispers.

My body screams in agreement as his voice turns up the intensity dial.

"Okay," I agree through heavy breaths.

"I'll go gentle. You stop me if it is too much," he says.

I nod as I feel him at the entrance. Slow little pushes as he takes my hips. My hands splay on the tree as the bark cuts into my palms. *Hold on. This might be a wild ride.*

I brace myself for the thrust, commanding my body to relax. The first is slow and gentle, just like he promised. Unwilling to tell him to stop unless there was pain I couldn't handle. The slow, shallow strokes continue, and I exhale. Willing my body to relax further. *Trust him.*

Pop. The sound of him going deeper. *He's inside me.*

"Oh my... " he breathes. The long, slow strokes, each one feeling deeper, and I continue to relax with how he fills me. *Not what I expected.*

"Take me, Drew," I say into the tree. My permission untethers him as he explodes inside me. Hands tighten around my torso. The unfamiliar sensation of how he finishes inside me is followed by him draping over my back. *A protective embrace.*

"Unfucking believable," he says as he slips out, and I hear his zipper.

I can't move, glued to the tree. My limbs will not listen to my brain, telling me to move. He helps get my shorts up before gathering me in his arms to turn me around. I collapse into his embrace, wetness dripping out of me. "Just a few scratches," he says, checking my neck. *That feels good, better than good.*

Heading back to the car, he holds my hand to lead me over rocks and branches. We were deeper in the woods than I thought, which reassures me no one likely witnessed my first anal experience in the wild.

He opens the passenger side door, and I awkwardly sit while he buckles me in. As he shuts my door, I open the glovebox, finding a napkin to shove into my shorts. Even though they are scratchy, it feels better not to be sitting in our fluids.

"Thank you for driving," I say, unable to wipe the smile of satisfaction from my face.

"Unbelievable. I'm not sure if I should say thank you... but thank you. You felt so good," he says.

I smile, not sure how to respond to that compliment. I've never heard that before, but I enjoy knowing his thoughts. It's reassuring.

"POP!" He smirks as he pulls onto the main road, and we head for home.

"We like trees!" I say, turning on the music. I'm so relieved I don't have to drive. My body feels completely relaxed.

DREW

I see Charley dozing off as I navigate the winding roads away from Lake Wiokka. "Why don't you put the seat back and rest your eyes?" I say, and before long, her body relaxes, and I wish I had a blanket to cover her up. She needs the rest after our forest adventure. Damn, that was fun. I love how willing she is to try things with me.

As I drive, the setting sun is pouring into Charley's window, picking up the hints of blonde and red in her brown hair that I never noticed before. Some strands have fallen on her face, and I want to move them so I can see her sleep, but I don't dare disturb her to rest. She needs it.

I had wanted to ask her if I could have her ass a few weeks ago when I noticed how she didn't shy away from me touching her while we played. But how do you ask someone that? Britt asked me and was eager for anal for as long as I remember. She was always up to try things, and I often went with the flow of her requests. A bit of a brat, but I knew how to tame her.

Charley is different. She's more submissive and needs to be led to surrender. It has been exciting to learn about her needs. I'm not sure how I got up the courage today to ask her, but the way she exposed herself to me was too perfect to pass up.

I admit the way the sun speckled down on her gave me the perfect view. I needed to see, to judge her willingness to take all of me. I take my eyes off the road and glance at her.

"Thank you," I whisper. Sliding myself inside her after she relaxed enough to let me in. *Heaven*. It only took a few thrusts before I exploded. I hoped for satisfaction and expected something like my previous experiences. *Didn't even come close.* How can being inside Charley feel so mind-blowing? *And she let's go!* Such a beautiful surrender.

She's perfect.

How did I not see this side of her before? A little vixen hidden inside the sweet girl-next-door façade.

I turn off the main road into Mountmooke Bay and down the side street to Gran's. The thought of what needs to be accomplished before the house goes on the market is overwhelming. Although Gran is feeling better, the plan is to sell the house and move to the family lake house in Brackenwood for next spring. Aunt Christine has agreed to go with her, which should work well since she and Uncle Christopher don't seem to see eye-to-eye regarding how to care for Gran. It's only forty-five minutes away, so Gran can still get to her medical appointments if needed. I agree with her plan, not that my opinion would change her mind. I think the lake air will be good for her for an entire season.

I've put in my papers to work at the local firehall. I knew changing jobs would happen soon since I can't live on my savings for much longer. After some calls, I found out they needed a new engineer. It's a bit of a pay difference from my old job, but the cost of living is better here, so it should all work out. I'm looking forward to having my own place again, just like my bachelor days. My space, my stuff... and enjoy Charley on every surface.

As I pull into the driveway, I hesitate. *Should I ask her to come in?*

"Charley, we're home," I whisper. Home. Maybe having a home with Charley wouldn't be so bad. I could carry her into our bed and watch her sleep. So peaceful... until I wake her up again for another round because I can't get enough.

"Charley, time to wake up," I say a little louder. She stirs.

"Oh sorry, I was out. I guess I wasn't good company on the way home." She clicks her seatbelt and gets out of the car. I follow, leaving the car running. *Time for her to go home.* I won't tempt her to stay.

Unless she will let you take her against the hood again.

The possibilities rush through my mind, wondering what we will do next. She wraps her arms around my waist, and I pull her in for a hug. She fits so nice against my chest, and I hear her take a deep inhale.

"You okay to drive home?" I ask.

"Oh yes, I'll be fine." She releases me and examines my face. "Thank you for today."

"The pleasure was all mine," I say, catching the smile making her face glow. *When do I get to have her again?*

She moves to get into her car, and I help with the door and make sure she is safe inside. "Talk later?"

"Always," she says as she shifts into reverse and backs out of the driveway. I feel a tug in my chest as she takes off down the street. I should have kissed her. Not that I would have known how to stop if I did.

Oh man, I'm in deep with that girl.

17

WHAT ABOUT MICHAEL?

CHARLEY

I walk to Margaret's back porch like I have so many Sunday afternoons, but things feel different today. Maybe it's because of my time with Drew yesterday? The memory of how our adventures took a completely new turn wakes up my core again. *This is not the time to think of such things.*

The box of wafer cookies in my hand sways as I stroll through the gate. Voices slow me down for a moment. *Is that the television?* Margaret rarely has it on so loud. I hear her laugh and then a male voice. *She has company.* Maybe I should turn around. I glance at my phone to check the time. *The time is correct.* Time for Sunday tea.

I take the steps to the back porch and turn the handle, determined to see who is there. I can always just drop off the cookies and let her visit in peace.

"Charley!" Margaret says in greeting as I open the door and look straight at Michael sitting beside her. *In my chair.* "Michael came for a visit. I didn't think you would mind if he joined us for tea?"

"Of course not," I blurt, waving off her concerns. What kind of person would I be if I said no? *One who forgot her manners?*

I notice Miss Camilla making a figure eight around my ankles. It's comforting in a strange way, like she knows I need the contact. I gather her in my arms and sit on the side stool. It's usually what Margaret uses to prop up her feet. She doesn't have a lot of space for a three person visit in this porch, but it is the best spot in the house to admire her garden, so I sit awkwardly with my knees above my hips. Miss Camilla, not liking how it's cramped in my lap, jumps out of my arms and races into the house. *Fine, go find a better spot.*

"Would you like to sit here?" Michael says, standing up from the chair beside Margaret. *My chair.*

"Oh, that is kind of you, Michael, but you stay right there." Margaret pats his arm, and he settles back into the chair. "You sit here, dear. Let me get the tea today." She rises slowly from her chair, and I jump to help her, making a mental note to talk to her later about a little wedge so she doesn't sit so low. I've noticed the last few times that she seems to struggle to get up. She lets me help her for a few steps but then swats me away.

"You sit and visit; I'm fine," she says as I glare at her.

This is new. She hasn't gotten the tea ready for years. It's my job. Then it hits me. *Magic Margaret the Matchmaker.* This is a setup. Damn it. How did I not see this from a mile away?

My mind races about what to do, but my body does as I'm told. I sit in her chair. As I lower myself, I notice how the cushion hugs my bottom, and I let out a sigh.

My ass needs softness today. I smile, realizing it doesn't matter that I lost my seat to Michael anymore.

My eyes track to the view from Margaret's vantage point. The beauty she has created is breathtaking. An explosion of colors. Tulips, peonies, and wildflowers grow together in a tangled embrace. *Why have I not noticed this before?*

"It is pretty, isn't it?" Michael says, breaking my thoughts.

I turn to him, but he isn't looking out the window. His eyes are on me and dipping down to my breasts as he licks his lips. *He's not subtle.*

"It's the month when everything seems in full bloom," I say, taking in his close-cropped hairstyle and clean-shaven face. His features are handsome with a sharp jawline and full mouth. I imagine for a moment if he is a good kisser. *Does he know Margaret is trying to see if we are a good fit?*

The heat rises in my cheeks slightly as I imagine what he would look like under the sports coat that seems to be tailored to fit him perfectly. A flutter of desire stirs inside me.

Remember Drew?

My mind shifts gears as I think about the problems this could present. *Drew is temporary.* Maybe Michael is supposed to be permanent. Should I let Margaret's efforts go to waste?

"Oh, the cookies," I say, bolting from the chair, remembering the bag I brought. "I should get this to Margaret for the tray."

"I can help; let you enjoy the view." Michael offers.

"That is very kind of you, but no. I'll be right back." I enter the kitchen and see Margaret sitting on a stool near the counter. The tray was empty in front of her. "I know what you are doing."

"Oh, and what's that, dear?"

I glance at her as I put the cookies on the tray.

She stands to put the kettle on.

"The kettle isn't on yet?" I ask.

"Well, I thought you could use some time together," she says as she pulls the cups from the cupboards. "You make a nice-looking couple."

I blush at that thought. "Well Miss Matchmaker, I hope we have more in common if you are going to all this trouble."

"Just get back out there and get to know him. Let me finish in here." She waves a hand to shoo me out. Rolling my eyes, I head back to the porch.

Michael is by the window, his height more noticeable now. I don't remember that from our meeting in the bookstore. He's taken off his sports coat and rolled up his shirt sleeves to show defined forearms, which lead to the most graceful-looking hands I've ever seen on a man.

"Can we have a peek outside while we wait for tea?" he asks, opening the door for me.

"That would be lovely," I say.

***

I wave goodbye to Margaret and Michael as I close the gate behind me. It's time for me to head over to see Drew, although I don't tell them that. I've lingered too long today. The tea was long gone, but the conversation was going so well I lost track of time. Now I'm late to see Drew.

I look at my phone, no messages. *He must be busy too.* As I head to my bedroom, I notice Troy isn't in his room. *Where is he?*

I rush to the washroom, eager to empty my bladder. I've been holding it the last half hour thinking teatime was almost over, but Margaret kept pulling me back into the conversation. Her matchmaking was better than I expected. Michael seems kind and can easily carry conversation. *And he's easy on the eyes.*

In other circumstances, I might have stayed longer, but the pull to see Drew won out.

> **Where are you?**

I text Troy as I freshen up my face and change into more comfortable clothes. Grabbing my purse and keys, I head to the garage.

> **I'm heading out for an hour. See you for supper?**

No response. Did I forget he had a game? I check the schedule. It's a practice.

> **Sorry, I just realized you are at practice. See you when you get home.**

Damn it. I used to be more in tune with his whereabouts. Does it mean I'm failing as a mother if I am not on top of things? *Of course not.*

I'm about to get into my car when I see Drew sauntering toward me, hands in his pockets.

"Hey," I say as I shut my car door.

"Hey, I know you said you were coming over, but when you were a no-show, I got concerned and came over."

"You didn't text?" I ask.

"I did, but you didn't answer. Sorry, I got a little worried. I know you had tea with Margaret, but I just got worried." He comes into my personal space and envelopes me in a hug.

"I'm sorry," I say as I notice his hug gets tighter. "I lost track of time."

"That's okay. I just needed to see you," he says.

"Drew, what's wrong?" I say, pulling out of his grasp. He lets out an enormous sigh.

"Gran and Aunt Christine came to the house today. It didn't go very well," he says.

"Oh, Drew, I'm so sorry. Let's go inside, and you can tell me what happened," I say, taking him by the arm and leading him inside. *He looks so defeated.*

I lead him to the kitchen, and before long, the story spills out. The plan was to sort things, but Aunt Christine insists there's no room, and Martha insists her memories need to go with her.

"I promised I would take anything she wanted to the Lake House, but honestly, I don't know how it is all going to fit. She wouldn't let anything go. They are both so stubborn!" he says.

"I can't imagine," I say, placing a cup of coffee in front of him. I would offer him a beer, but there is none in this house. Maybe I should stock what he likes to drink so I have it on hand.

"It's all too much. I needed to get out. I don't need to hear how donating the unicorn figurine is a disgrace to Gran's great aunt." He shakes his head and takes a sip.

"Is it hot enough? My coffee maker isn't the best," I add.

"It's wonderful. Thank you." He smiles at me as I sit across from him with my cup in hand.

I smile back, mostly because he came to me for some comfort. No matter how small it might be.

"How was Margaret today?"

"Oh! Well, I was a little blindsided when I arrived, and Michael was there."

"Michael? As in bookstore, Michael?" he asks.

"Yes! You remember." I laugh.

"Oh, I remember."

I don't miss the slight change in his tone with the comment. "Margaret is a determined matchmaker. We had a pleasant time." What else can I say? Does he want to know I find Michael attractive? Do I remind him we have a very specific arrangement and that it's temporary? *Why is my mouth so dry all of a sudden?*

I see he has a little twinkle in his eye as a little smile pulls at one corner of his mouth. I wonder if he is reading my mind again. *He knows.*

Do I tell him how I had to brush my inner dirty girl aside with Michael today? I couldn't help but wonder what it would be like if I knelt before him and asked to see all of him.

"What's running through your mind, Charley?" Drew asks.

"Nothing," I say, embarrassed.

"Liar," he says, leaning forward.

I bite my lip, knowing he is right. I am a big fat liar, and why do I have such a hard time shutting down these inner desires?

"Want to share?" He reaches out and strokes my fingers.

My body stirs, responding instinctively to the touch I know so well. *How does he always have this effect on me? Should I confess to Drew?* I stare at the coffee in my mug. Eyes down, thoughts overflowing. I drift into a fantasy world of 'what if?'. What if Michael and I are supposed to be together? What would happen to Drew? He would be okay. Would I be okay? *What is the right choice?* I barely know Michael; I need to stop jumping to a scenario of happily ever after. It doesn't exist.

"Charley?" Drew snaps me out of my trance, and I pull my hand away to take another sip. It doesn't matter that our arrangement is temporary. I want to be direct with Drew. So far, it's earned me a lot of pleasure, and I don't mind being summoned like a fuck toy. *Will Michael ever be able to pleasure me like Drew? Shut up.*

"You are blushing. I can't imagine what you are truly thinking." He leans back in the chair, filling the space with his body. It seems to take up the entire corner.

"Tell me how it would be if Michael joined us. Is that what you're thinking?" he asks.

I wasn't, but I am now! I perk up at the thought. A threesome. Well, how did he know I've had those thoughts?

"I think my mind got a little carried away, sorry," I say.

"Don't be sorry. I want to know your fantasies. Maybe I can make them come true?" *Make them come true! Who is this man?* The scenario plays in my mind.

"Well, I rarely talk about these things," I say.

"It turns me on to talk about them. No judgment. Tell me what you want, and maybe I can reward you later for being... descriptive," he says, stroking the coffee cup, making me want his fingers to do that to me.

"I, umm, how do I start?" I give my thoughts voice, and he shifts slightly, the tension clear in the way he adjusts, making no effort to hide the effect I have on him. My eyes widen. "You do like this," I say.

"You telling me your fantasies and maybe wanting to hear mine? Damn right. Tell me, Charley, I really want to know what is going on in that head of yours," he says, gesturing with his hand to have me continue talking.

I lean back and lick my lips, thinking of how he tastes in my mouth and the fantasy playing in my mind. *No judgement. Just tell him.*

"Well, I was thinking what it would be like to hold you both... in my hands," I say, gauging his reaction before continuing. His hand is on his thigh, and I follow the movement, noticing how close it is to his groin. Only a few movements and I could tug him free. "I could kneel before you both and take my time stroking and sucking," I say, and he lets out an airy breath.

"Well, that would be a sight I would like to see," he says.

"You would like to see if I can put both of you in my mouth?" I say and stand boldly, looking down at him. Willing myself not to kneel and take him right this moment.

"Oh God, yes," he says quietly. "I would try that with you." *I want the feeling of both men wrapped around my lips.*

I lean down and whisper in his ear. "I'm a naughty girl, and I want to show you what I could do with two men who are willing to let me have some fun."

He moans into my hair.

What am I saying? Unsure where that came from, I step away before I lose myself in this fantasy and start doing something to him in my kitchen. I open the pantry, looking for something, anything to distract me. I can't let my dirty girl take over right now. *She is not in charge.*

"Supper, what's for supper?" I say mindlessly to the cans.

"Trying to turn her off?" Drew says as he appears behind me. *How does he know?*

"No," I lie. "I need to figure out something for supper."

"Well, I was thinking you are the perfect meal for me," he says as he kisses my neck. *Give into him!*

"Hello!" I hear Margaret enter the back door, and Drew jumps back.

I grab a can of sauce and stand, meeting her eyes as she enters the kitchen. I can see Drew out of the corner of my eye rearranging items on the counter. *Damn it, we look guilty.*

"Hey Margaret, everything okay?" I ask, moving toward her and motioning for her to have a seat.

Drew turns and leans against the island, likely to hide the swelling in his pants.

"I didn't realize you had a visitor, Charley," she says, ignoring my question. Is that a tinge of judgement sprinkled in her tone?

"Oh, sorry. This is Drew. Martha's grandson."

"Drew! Oh yes. I know we haven't met yet, but Martha has told me so much about you."

"Good things, I hope," he says as he glances at me, asking for a lifeline.

"Of course. She was so proud when you made lieutenant at the fire station. Couldn't stop talking about it in our ladies' group," she says as she sits at the table and makes herself comfortable. Claiming her spot.

"Yes, that was a while back," Drew says as he shifts onto his other foot, not daring to come from behind the barrier.

"You left that job now? What are you planning to do for work?" Margaret asks.

Why do I feel like this is an interrogation?

"I have a new job at the fire hall in Ridgeport. Actually… I start next Monday," he says proudly.

I smile, wondering if he is eager to start the new job, but I'm happy he meets her questions with confidence.

"Well, that's lovely, dear. I guess we might see more of you around." It's not a question.

Drew and I glance at each other, knowing we will probably chat later about decoding Margaret's messages. She doesn't seem pleased he is here as her teeth clack together, tensing her jawline.

"Yes, well… I better get going. I have a few things to do before supper," Drew says as he heads to the door, and I notice the bulge has gone now. Thank God. "See you later. Nice to meet you, Margaret," he says, heading to the front door.

I want to follow him out and say a proper goodbye, but Margaret's stare glues me in place.

"He seems like a nice chap," she says, straightening her cardigan. Even with the increase in temperatures, she still wears one.

"Yes," I answer. *What else could I possibly say?* Any more information, and it could end up starting a conversation I can't finish. "How did the rest of your visit with Michael go?" I change the subject, hoping it'll work.

"Oh, isn't he just a darling? I saw the two of you hit it off well," she says. *Well? Hit it off? Did we? How do I answer?*

"Well, he was very nice. I enjoyed our visit," I say.

"I hope you don't mind. I gave him your phone number. I think you should spend more time with him," she says.

"Umm... okay," I answer, thinking I could block him if it gets weird.

"I know you tease me about being a matchmaker, but I don't want to see you alone anymore. You know I won't be around forever, and Troy goes off to college soon," she trails the last thought. Maybe hoping I will fill in the blanks.

"You don't want me to be alone?" I repeat.

"No." she nods her head.

"But I have friends. I'm not alone," I say defensively.

"Drew?" she asks.

"Well, yes. He is my friend," I say.

"Not the man for you," she says sharply. It sounds like I'm being scolded. *What? Where is this coming from?* "I know he's been hanging around you a lot. I don't like it. I want to see you with a man who can be a true partner. Drew has baggage, and HE is not the one."

"Baggage?" I ask. I don't know what else to say or how to take in all she's saying. *Make her stop.* Why is she so set on this all of the sudden?

"Yes, Troy needs a male in his life, someone who can be an excellent role model. Michael could do that. Why can't you give him a chance, dear?" Her tone softens slightly, and I know I need to give in. I will never win this argument.

"Yes, Margaret," I answer.

"Perfect. He is calling you tomorrow." She stands and turns to the door. "Say yes, dear, maybe he will be the perfect new husband you have been waiting for."

"Yes, Margaret," I repeat as she heads out the door. I put my head in my hands. What the hell just happened? Within fifteen minutes, my life has taken a turn I didn't see coming. Why is she so determined to find me a husband? What is up with her?

My mind flashes back to the conversation with Drew. He might not want a future with me, but he sure got turned on when I confessed my fantasy about a threesome. I wonder if Michael would be as willing to hear my fantasies too. *Likely not.*

"Hey, Mom!" I hear from the front of the house. *Supper. Damn it.* I haven't started supper. Well, with all this excitement, how can I focus on my mother duties? Failing in that department too, but not in your abilities to give Drew an erection. *Do they have a prize for that?*

"Hi, Troy, it will be ready in a moment," I shout back.

18

CBJ

CHARLEY

He's here. I breathe a sigh of relief as Drew pulls me into an embrace and the bell from the door rings again as the door closes behind him. *It's been a long seven days.*

"You're back," I say into his neck. His scent has a metallic twang but as he tightens his grip and lifts me slightly, I smell the familiar musk of Drew mixed with the citrus freshness of his white t-shirt.

"How come you're home early? I was just about to lock up," I say. It's five to four and most of my patrons do not do last-minute book buying, so I was cleaning before closing the store at four. His presence is a welcome surprise, but what is he doing home now?

"I've missed you," he says as he sweeps his tongue into my mouth and steals my next question. *I should lock the door.*

"They dismissed me at two thirty today, but I'm expected to be back before midnight. I took a night shift."

"A night shift? Is everything okay? Orientation was good? You like it?" I ask. *Too many questions.* I put my hands on his chest, trying to read his face. I'm happy he's home early, but now we only have a few hours. I was hoping we could have some fun tonight; every part of me is craving him. He nods and lifts me, my legs automatically wrapping around him. I cross my ankles behind his back. Effortless. I internally sigh at how much I enjoy the strength of this man.

"Everything is wonderful. I just needed to see you. You are done for the day? You can lock up?" he asks.

"I've missed you," I say between urgent kisses. "Yes, I can lock up now." But I make no move to do so as he growls in my ear.

"Good, we can hide in the back room?" He maneuvers with me wrapped around him, my eyes fluttering in anticipation. "I need your mouth, Charley."

I kiss him again as I take his face in my hands, and he ambles us into the back office. It's been too long. I need him too. My hands can't get to his belt and zipper fast enough as my feet find the floor. My hands tremble, fumbling slightly as he kisses and bites my neck.

"Is this a challenge?" I ask as I unzip his jeans while keeping my neck available for him. He growls again as I free him from his pants and start rubbing his length.

"See what you do to me?" he says. Is it possible for him to get harder with just those few strokes? He leans back on the desk, hands supporting him as I lower myself between his legs. *Damn, he is gorgeous.* My eyes drink him in as I pull his jeans and boxers down a little lower.

I glance at the office door. It's mostly shut, and I'm blocked from view behind this mountain of a man who has so politely asked for what he truly wants. *My mouth.*

I clasp his thighs as I open my mouth wide, tongue flat and slightly protruding. I take him in halfway before pulling back slowly as I smell something distinctly male mixed with the taste of salty sweat. My saliva coats his shaft as I refuse to use my hands; needed to turn my head, maneuvering him with my tongue for my pleasure. I close my eyes so I can use the touch of him to guide my movements.

"Charley," he moans.

I circle his tip with my tongue, teasing. Sometimes, it misses my mouth, and I feel the smooth skin stroke my cheek. Drool drips down my chin in anticipation. *How will he fit into my mouth?*

I open wide, leaving my hands on his legs to test how much my throat can take. Pushing him as far as I can without my hands. I bob back and forth, each time getting used to his length and pushing him farther until he hits the back of my throat. *Damn, that feels good.* A pulse of need runs through me, reminding me that my body wants more.

"Take all of it, Baby girl," he says in a ragged breath.

I move my hand to the base of his shaft as I pull back and inhale deeply. I didn't realize I had been holding my breath. I tilt up my head to look at him. *Baby girl?* I smile and stroke gently as a thread of spit connects his tip to my lips.

"Now that's a sight," he says.

I circle his tip with my tongue again, and a moan comes from my throat, low and animalistic. My hand continues to stroke as I take his tip and suck gently. The mix of sounds fills my ears, and my head buzzes from pleasure. Another moan, but I'm not sure if it's me or him. *Give me that sweet pre-cum.*

I try to clear my head as I hear his panting and feel him getting harder in my hand. I shift my mouth and take more of him, using my hand to slide up and down as he goes in and out.

"Oh, my god!" he says, tightening his stance and gripping the desk. His words make my confidence soar.

I want to take my time to savor it all. This is *mine*. *My toy*. My movements quicken as I worry I might not have much longer before he stops me. Last time, he grabbed my arms and lifted me so he could bend me over to finish. Will that happen again?

The memory sends a warmth spreading through me. I pull my hand away and devour his length, pushing past the gag reflex and testing my limits. I part my lips and make a slight movement, feeling soft taps at the back of my throat. I hold on just before I feel the reflex, wanting to give in.

Time slows as I pull back and use my tongue to squeeze his tip with my palette. The sensation lights my fire.

"Oh my... gawd... I'm so close."

My inner dirty girl sits back to bask in her glory as I repeat the motion, and his moan fills the room. *I need to finish him like this.* I need this. He needs this.

I use both hands, stroking his base and cupping his balls. I hold my breath as I take him as deep as possible, and as I start to pull him out slowly, I use my tongue to press into his length. He explodes in my mouth, but I don't stop.

"Oh my god, oh my good god," he says. His hands in my hair, pulling slightly to tell me to stop. *I will not stop until I am ready.*

I slow my licks so I can hold the mouthful of his release. I lean my head back and open wide to show him.

"Swallow that," he commands. I swallow and smile, licking my fingers like I've just had a gourmet meal. *Fantastic.*

After his pants are fastened, I notice he won't stop staring at me.

"What was that?" he asks.

"You like?"

"Of course, you just... you've never done it like that before," he says. He must be full of post-release hormones. Everything must feel good after your dick has been sucked.

"I'm glad you liked it," I say with a smirk. *I know he loved it.* Hard to fake that kind of pleasure.

He grabs my face with both hands, forcing me to look at him. *What is he doing? Is he upset? Why does it feel like he's looking into your soul?*

"Your skills are something I've never seen or felt before. You are one of a kind, and I love I get to experience you like this."

My heart pounds at the intensity of his words. *Praise for the dirty girl.* He is dialing her in, and she sits at attention, taking in each syllable. *She doesn't want to hide anymore.*

"I don't want you ever to think you are too much or not enough. You are exactly who you are supposed to be. I'm so glad I get to witness this part of you. You are AMAZING!" he says as he holds me in a firm embrace.

Don't cry. I smile and nod into his shirt, hoping he won't notice. I'm trying so hard to fight the tears, but it's no use. He hit a chord within me that's no longer a secret. I need this side of me to be seen.

I inhale, trying to calm my emotions as he holds me by the shoulders at arm's length, examining my face. My eyes fall to his chest as he strokes my cheeks, wetness smearing. He takes my chin, and I'm forced to look at his eyes. A hiccup, half cough, escapes my throat. *I need to compose myself.*

"You are amazing," he says and kisses the wetness on my cheeks.

"It's only you. You drive me wild," I giggle, hoping the playful words will hold back my tears. "Well, your BJs are something special," he says, kissing my other cheek and then full on the mouth. *He must be able to taste himself.* My mood shifts at the realization, and I want to ask him if he likes the taste as much as I do.

"CBJs!" he cries out in a laugh, breaking my thoughts.

"A what?" I ask.

"A CBJ. You have your own special talent. I can give it a name if I want."

"Yes, you can," I say, shaking my head but smiling at his silliness. He kisses my forehead, his lips lingering. I breathe deeply, trying to identify all the scents now lingering on me and him.

"Mom!!" I hear Troy's call, and my panic rises. *Oh no.* Am I dressed? *Yes, I'm dressed.*

"Mom!" A more urgent call, and I see him open the door to the office.

"I'm in here," I say, not that he needs this information at this moment.

"What the hell?" Troy says.

"Watch your language, son," I scold.

"What is he doing back here? What are *you* doing back here?"

I glare at Drew, and I stand between them. Feeling protective.

"He's here to see me," I say.

"Oh ya? I think he is doing more than looking!" Troy's temper rises with his tone. "Mom, you aren't supposed to be hanging out with Drew anymore," he says in a half whine that makes me want to shake my head to dislodge the words.

"What? Why?" I say. *Where the hell is that coming from?*

"Margaret said you were done with him," he says, pointing a finger.

"Your mom and I are friends, Troy. Is it okay if I come to visit her?" Drew's tone is low and calm. *How is he staying calm right now?*

"Well, she was supposed to meet me half an hour ago. So, no, Drew, I guess it's not okay." Troy's anger flares.

This is going terribly wrong. *At least he didn't arrive ten minutes ago.*

"I just got back. I'm sorry I kept your mom busy. I'll head out." Drew says.

"No, that's okay," I say and look at Troy turning my back on Drew so I can feel the strength of him behind me. "Troy, I'm sorry I was late. We can go shopping for jeans tomorrow," I say as calmly as possible.

"It's fine Mom, let's just go home. Please," Troy says, rolling his eyes.

Normally, I wouldn't tolerate that from him, but I'm just happy he calmed down a little. This could have been so much worse.

Drew motions a goodbye, and I so desperately want to kiss him and tell him I'll see him soon, but there is no way I can show Troy that side of our friendship. I'm torn as I watch Drew leave the bookstore. *Switch into mom mode.*

"What time does Kirkman close?" I ask, grabbing my purse. Maybe we have time to get him the jeans I promised.

"I want to go home, Mom. PLEASE," Troy says.

"Fine," I say, locking the store behind me. We get to the car, and it's a quiet ride home. My mind fills with questions and what ifs. Stupid of me not to lock the door. What if Troy found me on my knees giving a BJ?

A CBJ. I smirk at that thought. What is wrong with me?

Troy is on his phone, so I figure he likely can't see my reactions as I mull over the last hour of my life. What did he mean about Margaret?

"Troy?" I say, hoping it will get him to stop texting and listen to me. It doesn't. "What did you mean Margaret said I was done with Drew?" I ask.

"Huh? What?" he says, barely looking up from his phone. I take a breath and repeat myself.

"Oh, she said you liked Michael now, and he might be my new stepdad. I like him. He's nice," he adds.

"He's nice? You met him?" I ask.

"Ya, Margaret introduced me after church before you had your tea thing with her," Troy says.

What? Oh my god. It is so much worse than I thought. "Well, Drew is my friend, but I don't understand why you don't like him," I say, hoping he will tell me more.

"It's not that I don't like him. I just know he won't be here very long."

So much information. *So many questions.* It's rare for Troy to be talking so much, so I am doing my best to keep my tone calm.

"Well, he got a new job. He's not going back to Denver," I say, and Troy shrugs.

"Well, doesn't he have a fiancé back there? I know he's your 'friend' Mom, but let's not forget that she's around," he says, and my grip tightens on the steering wheel. *Where did he hear all of this?* Margaret, it has to be Margaret. She is not a matchmaker; she is a puppeteer. What the hell is happening? When did she become so involved in my life like this? The sweet ole lady façade is over!

"Mom, I'm not stupid. I know you like Drew more than a friend. We are just looking out for you," he says, glancing at me and then back at his phone. I'm glad he can't see the anger I'm stuffing down. *What... the... fuck.*

"Thank you, sweetheart. I know you are," I say, trying not to drip sarcasm. *You can't look out for me if you don't know what I want.* What the hell am I going to do?

19

GREEDY ASS

DREW

My orientation is finally over. Charley and I have talked on the phone a few times. She seems to be concerned about when Troy saw us in the bookstore the other day. I tried to reassure her, but I'm just not sure what else we can do. She wants our relationship to remain a secret, which comes with some consequences.

Unfortunately, the one mainly in our faces is Margaret playing matchmaker.

Part of me wants to laugh at the attempt, and the other part of me wants to convince her we have moved past this friends-with-benefits stage. My gut wrenches at the thought of not having her in my life. Maybe someday she will feel the same way.

We're going apartment hunting today since I've decided it's time to find a place of my own. Gran is finally settled back at Aunt Christine's. The house is staged, and the for-sale sign is up. I don't feel like it's my home anymore. Gran has moved on, now, so can I.

I pull into her driveway and secretly hope Troy isn't here. I don't know how to handle a sixteen-year-old, even though I was one a long time ago. Maybe he's just being protective of his mom? *Join the club.* That's how I feel all the time. Go away, Michael!

"Hello?" I enter Charley's house, and silence greets me.

"I'm in here... alone." She calls from the other room. *Alone?*

I round the corner and see Charley standing, holding a shiny object like a prized possession. Her hands are cupped, offering it to me as a toothy grin splits her face. "I got us a present."

"A present?" I ask, sauntering toward her. I haven't seen her in five days. Driving here, I was feeling tired after my last shift. It's been a lot of new things to learn, and it makes my head hurt to remember it all. But seeing her like this, I get a second wind.

"No one is here... or next door." She waggles her eyebrows, the cuteness overflowing. Maybe she is hoping it is sexy in some sort of strange way, but the cuteness overpowers her movements, and I have to bite the inside of my cheek not to laugh.

"Did you make that happen?" I ask, moving closer to see what she is holding.

"I did. I want to play. Want to play?" She asks. *Damn.* The cute, sexy swirls together, and the need to touch her takes priority. Taking her face in my hands, I kiss her roughly.

"Yes." I breathe.

"I've missed you," she says, wrapping her arms around my neck and I feel the cool touch of whatever she had in her hand. Damn it, now I need to see. A thrill shudders through me.

"What's in your hand, Charley?" I ask.

"A new toy for us to play with." She puts it in front of my face, a little too close for me to see. I lean back, and she pops it into her mouth. I see a flash of pink sparkle before she pops it back out with two fingers. *Butt plug. Fuck me.* My body reacts at the thought of how it will look inside her.

"I'm going to go put this in my ass," she says.

"No wasting time," I laugh.

"I've been excited all day; we have a small window. Let's make the best of it. Be right back. Meet me in the bedroom?" She says before sticking the end in her mouth again and sucking it like a ring pop. I nod in agreement. I love that there is no hard-to-get routine.

She wants to play.

I strip down and rub myself. Not that it needs much encouragement. I'm going to enjoy this. *Let's play.*

CHARLEY

Of course, he said yes. We don't play games; he likes it when I'm direct. I smear lube on the plug and gently insert it. Well, that's not the sensation I was expecting.

I wiggle. Maybe I should have tried it beforehand. *Deep breath, relax. There, that is better.*

As I walk into the bedroom in only my t-shirt, the sensation of fullness runs through my body, turning into pleasure. I close the bedroom door, and I drink at the sight of Drew standing naked in front of me. *Admire this beautiful man.*

He grabs me playfully and kisses me hard. Hands grab my ass cheeks, lifting me toward the bench at the end of the bed. The plug shifts, and I clench as I kneel, not wanting to sit and disturb the novel sensation.

"I like naughty Charley," he says as a little giggle bubbles out of my mouth. The waves of relaxation take over as he explores my body. He pulls my shirt up and tugs at my nipples with his teeth. Bending low so I can see his back muscles shift as he finds his mark.

"I missed these," he says between nibbles. With both hands on one breast, he sucks with a force that makes me gasp. His hand roams to my waist and leans back as he continues to kiss my body.

Now on his knees, he parts my legs, and they open willingly for his mouth to land on me. "So wet for me," he says as I gasp again, flexing my hips to give him better access.

My mind wants to focus on one thing at a time, but I'm not having any luck. He pushes into me, so I lean back and put my hands on the bed, exposing myself to him as his tongue circles my sensitive center.

"Oh my God," I say, knowing I'm climbing fast. Unsure how I can slow this down and savor it some more. *Hold on, it's going to be a wild ride.*

"Turn over, I want to see." He slaps my thigh lightly, and I go on all fours awkwardly. Feeling like Bambi, no grace in my limbs.

"Well, that is pretty." He grabs the jewel and turns it a little. I squirm at the sensation, not wanting to move away from him. I tense, concerned how to handle how this little movement turns on every nerve. He moans, and I go on my forearms, resting on the bed as my legs spread on the bench and raise my rear in the air.

"There is the view I want." He nips at my ass cheek, and I surprise myself by not flinching. *Pleasure and pain. I want to ride this boundary.* I relax again as he bends lower to tug on the plug a little.

"You like that?" he asks.

"Oh god, yes!" I say just as his tongue swipes lower. My legs shake, unsure if they will hold me in this position before I collapse in satisfaction. *Hold on a little longer.*

The orgasm builds fast as he moves the plug in and out in little, quick movements. I scream my pleasure into the blankets. Happy they can muffle the sound.

The sensations relax me further, and I am ready for the crash that will happen soon. *Just let go.*

Then he stops.

What happened? Where is he?

"Umm... I lost it," he says as he places a hand on my hip to get my attention. In my daze, I take a moment to get the thoughts formed in my mind and out of my mouth.

Lost it? What? What is he talking about?

I turn around, and I can see his panicked face. "It just went... umm... inside," he says. I spread my legs to feel inside. *Yup, it's in there.*

My finger hits the jewel part; it is just at the surface. It's like I've swallowed it up. He watches me as I spread my legs wider and reach inside, curling my finger until I get around the edge.

"I got it," I say in an overly cheery voice. No embarrassment. It's my body.

His eyes are wide as he witnesses my mission of pulling the jewel out and exposing it to him again.

"We can leave the other part in?" I ask because there is no reason we can't continue.

"You just did that like it was nothing," he says.

I nod since I can't find the right words.

"You amaze me, Baby girl, goddamn." He pulls me closer and kisses me roughly, laying me down on the edge of the bed. He moves inside me, and I gasp at the overwhelming sensation of being completely filled. "Oh, my god!" I scream.

"I can feel it," he says as he continues to thrust, slowing down to take in the sensations.

My mind numbs as the orgasm comes fast. I crash into the waves of my release, unsure how to quantify the amount of pleasure this is giving me right now.

"I never thought it could feel like that." He sways, collapsing on top of me as he catches his breath.

I don't want to think about how much time we have left. I wish we could just stay like this a little longer and not go back to our lives and all our other responsibilities.

Can't I just live in this Drew bubble a little longer? I feel him slip out of me, and I know time is up. *Back to reality.*

20

MISS MATCHMAKER MARGARET

CHARLEY

I am here. As the stale smells and floral perfume hit me, it affirms how much I want to flee. But I'm here at Grace Community Church because Margaret needs me. I had a weak plan to tell her I was sick. *That wouldn't work. You can't fool her.* She arrived by my house an hour before the service, telling me her hip was hurting, and she didn't want to drive today. How can I say no to this woman?

As we walk by the large oak doors, she insists on taking my arm. "Just help me to my spot, dear."

"Of course." My words get cut off by her friend, who greets her with a big hug.

"Margaret, I'm so happy to see you," she says as I get pulled a little too much into the awkward hug because Margaret refuses to let my arm go. I scan the pews as she continues with her pleasantries. *My spot is taken.* I guess if you don't come for a few weeks, that can happen. My eyes wander to Margaret's spot, and I see there is room for me there. Not much. We better hurry before it gets gobbled up with parishioners.

"I'll see you tomorrow for bible study?" The lady says to Margaret as we move away from her. Margaret's politeness is always present with her church ladies. I can't help but tuck away the detail that she will have Bible study tomorrow. If she is gone, maybe Troy has a practice, and Drew can come over to play. *We are in church! Such sinful thoughts.*

We make it to Margaret's pew, and she doesn't say a word, just expecting me to sit with her today, I guess. Maybe she noticed my spot was taken?

She lets go of my arm and waddles down to her spot. I follow, noting how she is favoring her leg a bit more. Maybe I should tell her we need to go get it checked. As she plunks herself down, I freeze. The open spot is between her and Michael. *God damn it.*

"Hi Charley, nice to see you again," he says as I sit and adjust the hem of my skirt, so my knees are hidden. *How did I not notice he was there?*

"Well, this is a surprise," I say, trying not to glare at Margaret, the puppeteer. We will have something to discuss at tea this afternoon. *Unless she has invited him? So many questions, and how do I get my answers in a place like this? God damn it!* Is it bad to take the lord's name in vain, even if it's only in my head? I wonder if it's worse because I'm in church. *Damn. I'm going to hell.*

"I heard the choir has been practicing for a special performance today," Michael says.

I nod and look at Margaret.

"Yes, I thought he would enjoy that. Of course, you would know what was happening if you hadn't missed four weeks," Margaret whispers into my shoulder. I want to correct her and say it was three, but I don't think it matters, so I purse my lips shut. *I will never win an argument with her.*

I glance sideways at Michael, trying not to be obvious. I'm a little taken aback by the way he looks so comfortable in his perfectly tailored suit. *How is that possible?* Doesn't everyone look uncomfortable in church? *Not him.*

I try not to stare at the way the cuffs of his shirt poke perfectly out of his sleeves. His hands gently resting on his thigh. I wonder what they would feel like on my body. *Did I just go there?*

Handsomeness is not so easily ignored. Those little details of his body interest me in a way I wish they didn't. The tapping of his fingers on his thigh catches my attention. *Maybe he's nervous?* I adjust my posture, and he glances at me with a sideways smile. Relief fills me at his slight discomfort. I nod back. *At least he's not a robot.*

The service drags on, and the choir performance is fine, but nothing to write home about.

Margaret takes my hand during the last prayer. "I'm so happy you are here today," she whispers as everyone says AMEN in unison.

"I am too." I kiss her cheek and see her eyes tearing. This soft side of Margaret knows how to soothe the awkwardness that has been racing through me sitting so close to Michael.

I wonder if others noticed the seating arrangement. Maybe Margaret let her friends from the ladies' group in on her matchmaking efforts. I glance at Michael again. *Maybe he is the man I need in my life?* Maybe I need to trust Margaret and see if he checks the boyfriend boxes I created in my mind. I should give him a chance. There was just one issue niggling at me. *He's not like Drew.*

But what does that even mean? How do you put it into words? And why am I even comparing them? Maybe it would be nice to come to church with Michael and build a life of service in the community. *Is that me?* It could be.

The service concludes with murmured voices that get louder as the organ starts a song to send us on our way. Margaret takes my arm again and starts introducing us to an older woman who was in front of us.

"Yes, this is Michael. My cousin's grandnephew on my mother's side. You know Charley?" she says.

"Hi, nice to meet you," I say, shaking her hand because I'm not sure I remember meeting her, and I don't want to forget my manners.

"Hi Charley, yes, we met a few months ago," she says, and I blush. *Damn it.* What is her name again? I've already forgotten.

Michael compliments her hat, and his politeness takes the focus away from me. I sigh in relief.

As we make our way out of the church, Margaret and I arm in arm and Michael at our backs as a protective six-foot wall; I suddenly wonder how this became my life. Was I not just Drew's dirty whore yesterday afternoon? *This is not me.* What am I doing? Just try!

***

It is time for tea, and I'm in my kitchen getting the cookies to take over for Margaret. I found some vanilla wafers at the store this week and know she will enjoy them. I'm trying to figure out how to get through this next hour with Michael, only to tell Margaret this will never work. *Will she understand?*

How do I explain she can't interfere with this part of my life? I check my phone and see I have messages from Drew.

> Hope church went okay. Can't stop thinking of yesterday. You know how to take it all in stride!

> Just about to start my shift. I'll check texts when I can. Have a nice time at Margaret's today. I know you love your visits. Enjoy.

> Just heading over now. Church was okay.

I type about Michael being at church and delete the text. How do I describe this via text? I linger over the keypad and decide this is not a text conversation. I'll tell him about Margaret the Matchmaker later.

> Have a good shift. Talk soon.

I stick my phone back in my purse as guilt oozes from me. *What am I doing?* Drew and I are friends. Period. I need to figure out what to do about Michael. I sigh, grabbing the cookies.

"Halloo?" a voice as the door opens and closes.

"Margaret? I've got the cookies. Sorry, I'm a few minutes late. Everything okay?" *What is she doing here?*

"Hello dear, I just wanted to have a chat with you privately before you came over for tea," she says.

"Oh? So, Michael is joining us?" I ask, playing along.

"Yes, he will be along shortly, but I need a moment with you. Where is Troy?" She asks.

"He's in the living room watching a show. Is everything okay?" Wondering why I can't read her properly. Am I getting bad news? *Did I upset her?* I can't tell.

"Oh good, hopefully he can't hear us." She sits at the table in her usual chair. *Don't panic. Just let her talk.*

I move a chair closer to her so she can lower her voice if needed. "I know you seem shy with Michael, but I have it on good authority that he is very interested in getting to know you and Troy better. I think he might ask you out on a date. I want you to say yes."

"But I," I stammer.

"No buts, I don't know exactly what you have been doing with this Drew guy, but I don't like it. It's time you think about this seriously. Michael is a good man, and you deserve a good man," she says, taking my hand.

"I want what is best for you, and I can feel it in my gut that you are not meant to be alone forever. Troy will be off to college, and then what? I want you to give Michael a proper try. Please, for me." Her voice cracks.

I don't have the heart to fight her anymore. Maybe she is right? Drew and I are fuck buddies; that's not forever. "Michael is a nice man," I say.

"But?" she says.

"No buts. I'm sorry I've not given him a chance. I'll do better, Margaret." I lean over and kiss her cheek. How can I argue with a woman who only wants what is best for me? *And what if she is right?* We leave my kitchen to head over to her house for tea and I expect Michael will be along shortly.

"There he is," she whispers to me as we open the gate. "You go say hello, and I'll start the tray."

I hand her the cookies and nod. Her matchmaking skills are getting more and more refined.

Michael's back is to me as he sits on the bench facing the hydrangeas, one of my favourite spots. He took off his suit jacket and rolled up his sleeves, exposing his forearms. One is draped on the back of the bench and as I round the path to face him, he smiles in a big, toothy grin. My heart melts at the welcoming sight.

"Come have a seat?" he asks. The invitation feels harmless, but my inner dirty girl betrays me as she imagines what it would be like to curl up beside him. I need to get these thoughts in check.

"Thank you," I say, noticing he doesn't move his hand, so I'm entering his personal space. "It is lovely here, isn't it?"

"Beautiful," he says, looking at me in a way that makes my cheeks flush. "I was hoping we might have a moment to ourselves today."

"Oh?" I prompt. My nerves kick in as I imagine all the things he could say next. What if he asks me something I don't want to answer? *Then we don't answer.*

"Yes, I know. Margaret seems to push us together a bit. I don't know if you have been feeling that too?" he asks, moving down the bench a little to make a little more room for me. I turn to face him, playing with the hem of my dress so it covers my knees. *Why am I so concerned he will see my knees?*

"Yes, I can only apologise. I know she seems to think I'm not capable of doing this on my own. If you want me to talk to her, I can," I say into my lap. My hands now grasped so hard together to capture the embarrassment. I'm mortified at his observations.

"Charley," he says, shifting a little closer. "I was hoping maybe we can tell her it worked. I would like to take you out for supper. Get to know you better, not just from what Margaret tells me."

It has been so long since a man talked to me like this. My shyness pushes toward his formal politeness. "That would be lovely."

He takes my hands in his, and I soften at his warm touch. His kindness overflows to ease whatever walls I seem to put up. I'm not sure what this is all about. *He's a nice man. Give him a chance.*

I need to tell Drew.

21

WHERE PATHS DIVIDE

DREW

I call Charley as soon as I find a free moment. The station has me hopping from back-to-back calls and I finally sat to get some grub. I dial again, but it goes to voicemail. She must be with customers.

> **Call me if you can. So much happening can't text it all.**

I need to hear her voice. *Am I allowed to tell her that?*

My new job has me as the operator for Fire Engine Three, and I'm still learning her tricks. When I arrived on the scene earlier today, the hydraulic system failed. It took almost five minutes for me to make the adjustments and repairs to get the ladder for the crew. I need to go back and run a complete diagnostic on the truck, so it won't happen again. The captain didn't give me a hard time about it. He knows Engine Three needs some repairs.

My phone vibrates on the table, and I eagerly grab it, leaving my food half-eaten and head to a private spot. Not easy to find.

"Hey, stranger!" I say, tapping the button to accept the call.

"I'm sorry, Drew, I was with a customer and didn't see your call. Are you okay?" She sounds tired and exhausted.

"All is well, just a lot happening, and I hadn't been able to text." I want to say more, but I can hear voices in the background.

"Oh, that's okay. I know you are busy. I'm keeping myself busy too." I hear a muffled, "I'll be right with you." *Damn it.* My timing sucks.

"When are you home?" she asks.

"Not until Friday," I say. Guilt floods me. I hate I can't see her until then.

"Oh, I thought you had Wednesday off?" she says with a hesitation in her voice.

"Yes. I do, but it's such a quick turnaround. I think I'll stay here and work on the truck. Jimmy will be here, and we can be faster with some repairs if I stay to help." I say, not wanting to add how I want to give my truck some TLC. No more five-minute delays on my watch.

"Oh, of course. I have a customer waiting. Sorry, Drew, I can't talk long," she says. The disappointment in her voice makes a lump form in my throat. The life of a firefighter. *This is what Britt didn't like either.* I know we're not a couple, but I want Charley as part of my life. *How do I make room for her?*

"What if you come to Ridgeport after work on Wednesday? I can take you out to eat. I need some actual food, and I would enjoy the company," I say.

"Can I let you know Wednesday morning? I just want to check in about Troy first," she says.

"Of course. Talk soon?" I ask.

"Yes, talk so... " the call disconnects. Well, that's not like Charley. Something is off. It must be she has a customer. No, it's her tone. *Something is wrong.* I can feel it in my gut.

CHARLEY

I can't think straight. The store is so busy, and I feel like my brain is going to explode. My restless night's sleep, plus trying to sort out how to tell Drew. I thought he would be home this week. *Damn it.*

I serve the next customer and check Troy's game schedule. Wednesday is practice; that's all I needed to know.

I know his reply will come when he can. *It's time to tell him.* Time to end this situationship. *Find the words.*

***

My Tuesday at the bookstore dragged on. Usually, those days I read, but my mind is on Drew and Michael. The back and forth. I know what I need to do. *Just do it.* I have been practicing how to tell him and try to keep our friendship intact. *That was the deal.*

The voices get louder as I open the front door to my house. Shoes litter the front entrance. I can barely open the door. One, two, three... five pairs of sneakers that don't look familiar. Troy asked to have a friend over, but I didn't expect this.

"Fuck, yah, dude!!" I hear from the living room. Troy never does this, and I know he will leave for college, and I will miss it. *Let him be.*

I don't need to interrupt the boys, so I decide to sneak out the back door to check on Margaret. It seems like the best solution to distract myself from thoughts of Drew.

"Hello dear," Margaret says from the back porch as I open the gate. "Troy has some friends over, I see."

"You noticed?" I say, finding my way to my chair beside her.

"Hard not to. They seem to all come at once. He seemed so happy to have them arrive; I just couldn't interrupt."

"I feel the same way. It's kind of nice to have the house full of laughter." I sigh, putting my head back.

"Long day, dear?" she asks.

"Yes," I want to tell her more, but I don't want to burden her with my problems. After a few pauses, Miss Camilla saunters into the room and rubs against my leg in a silent message, telling me to relax. I reach down and pick her up, feeling her fur between my fingers and taking a breath. *Better tell her about Michael.*

"I'm not sure if you know, but Michael and I have tentative plans to go for dinner this Saturday," I say.

"Really?" she says. I'm not sure if it's genuine. *Maybe she knew?* Miss Camilla jumps off me to sit with Margaret. Pushing her head into Margaret.

"Miss Camilla has been sticking very close to me today. She doesn't seem to stop doing this," she says, gesturing to how the cat is rubbing into her chest, working her way up to her neck. It's not gentle and looks aggressive.

"She's not been this demanding before. Maybe something is wrong with her head? Should I take her to the vet? Can you come with me?" she says, trying to calm Miss Camilla into her lap.

"Of course," I say, noticing the change in topic. Miss Camilla continues to rub her head vigorously on Margaret's neck as she whispers softly.

"It's okay, my sweet," she says to the cat before turning to me. "Maybe she just needs more attention today," she says, and I see the way Miss Camilla is on Margaret. She's right; it's not her usual behaviour. *But Miss Camilla is not a usual cat.*

"Let's go into the garden. I want to show you the Azaleas. Something seems to be attacking them, and I can't figure it out," she says. I raise from my chair and help Margaret from the affectionate ministrations of Miss Camilla by taking her into my own arms. She appears frightened at this change and jumps down, skittering out her little door in the corner to the yard.

"Thank you, dear. Now, she will find another spot until I call her for supper."

As we stroll through the garden, she tells me all about each plant. I never tire of her reviewing inventory with me. I have learned a lot over the years. My garden isn't as expansive, but it's lush because of Margaret's lessons.

"I think we need to split all of this next year," she says, pointing at the hostas in the side yard. "Would you be okay to put them along your driveway? It would make a delightful spot for them."

"That's a great idea," I say, taking her hand. "Margaret, are you feeling okay?" I notice beads of sweat are forming on her lip. It's not hot enough for her to perspire today; maybe we've been out too long. I should take her in.

"I'm fine," she says, patting my hand. "Let's go see how many hostas we can fit." She holds my hand as we head toward my front yard.

She wastes no time pacing out seven feet. Accuracy doesn't seem to matter as she announces, "We can fit at least ten."

I notice her breath comes out in huffs. "Margaret? Are you okay?" I ask again.

"I just can't... my breath," she pants.

"Let's go inside and sit," I say, leading her to the kitchen. As I guide her to the chair, I feel her blouse is damp, and the sweet odour of her sweat wafts toward me.

"I don't feel very well," she says as I go for my phone in my purse. I notice I have multiple text messages but now is not the time. "I think you need to call the doctor."

I dial 9-1-1 and scream for Troy.

"Hello, 9-1-1. What is your emergency?" The speaker says on my phone. I relay my name and address just like I have seen in the shows. *Is that what you do in real life?*

"My neighbour is here, and she doesn't feel well. She's sweating and can't catch her breath." I put my phone to my chest to muffle the sound and scream again, "Troy!"

No answer. Where is he?

"Margaret, I'm going to lay you down," I say, helping her to the floor. *Oh god, is this a good idea?*

"The paramedics are on their way. Keep talking to me, Charley. Is Margaret talking to you?" I hear the lady say on the phone.

Margaret's eyes roll in her head, and she shakes.

"Oh my God! She's shaking. She's SHAKING! What do I do? Is that a seizure? Oh my god, it's a seizure. What do I do?" I say as my head buzzes.

"Just make sure she can't hurt herself. Move things out of the way." The voice says calmly as I put the phone on speaker and lay it on the floor.

"I've put the phone on speaker," I shout as I move the chair that was close to her legs. I try to push the table, but I'm not having any luck. *Troy, where is Troy?*

I look down the hall to the front door. No shoes. They are gone. *I'm alone.* No, I'm not alone. I have Margaret and the lady on the phone.

"Can you tell me if she is breathing?" the voice says.

"I can't tell. The shaking has stopped now. How can I tell if she is breathing?" I say and put my hand on her chest to feel for a heartbeat. *Is that how you do it?* I should have paid more attention to those rescue shows. Her large breasts shoved into a far too small bra seem to make it impossible for me to gain access. *Do I take off her top? She would be mortified.* I wish Drew was here. He would know what to do.

"Put your... " the voice says, but I cut her off.

"I can hear her breathing! She is breathing!" I shout, relief running through me.

"The ambulance is almost there; can you make sure the door is open for them? Margaret is okay if you leave her." The voice says.

"Okay, yes." I stand, realizing I've been splayed out on the floor beside her. Dirt covers my pants, and I curse myself for not passing the broom earlier. *How am I criticizing my housecleaning skills right now?* I look at Margaret. She looks like she is resting on the floor. *This is not okay. She's not okay.*

I race to the front door, hearing sirens, knowing they are close. I open the door and hesitate with the handle in my hand. *Do I wait? Do I go to Margaret?*

Margaret wins.

"Margaret, the paramedics are here. They are going to look after you," I say as I crouch down beside her again. *Dirty pants and all.* I smooth her hair and kiss her cheek.

"You are okay. Everything is going to be okay." I look and notice her face looks strange and slack. *What the heck!*

"Hello Charley? We are here for Margaret. Can you please step aside so we can make our assessment?" I hear him, but it doesn't compute.

"Something is wrong! You need to help!" Blood rushes to my ears, and my head spins as someone helps me to my feet and urges me to come with her. I see a man over Margaret and mouthing words, I can't hear them. He opens her blouse with scissors. Oh god, she loves that shirt, she will be so upset.

Someone is pulling on my hand, and I turn toward them. Michael.

22

UNCOMFORTABLY NUMB

CHARLEY

I can't move. It's comfortable in this spot, or maybe it's just that I don't want to move. If I don't go into Grace Community Church, then maybe I can go back home and see Margaret.

That's what I want to do. Pretend all of this is a bad dream, and when I go home, I'll head over to Margaret's through the back gate, and she will be there in her chair.

It has been seven days since I saw her on the kitchen floor. I couldn't scrub it clean enough to wipe the image from my mind. My house is cursed. What do I do? I don't know what to do.

Michael takes my hand. "Come on now, Charley, let's go say our goodbyes." *Goodbyes?* How do you say goodbye? I shake my head, and the tears form, threatening to fall.

"I don't know how," I mutter.

"Troy, take your mother's hand," Michael says as I get out of the limo. My hand in Troy's, feeling the solidness of his hand that feels larger somehow. *He's grown up so fast.*

On impulse, he left the day Margaret had her episode in our kitchen. I can't say she died. *Not yet.* Troy left the house moments before we were measuring the flowerbed. Another friend had texted him, and the group of boys headed off to play a game of basketball.

Thank goodness for small mercies. I'm grateful he wasn't there to witness the paramedics trying to restart

Margaret's heart but telling him about the episode nearly broke my heart as he collapsed on the floor and cried. No one prepares you for that as a mother. He has shed no tears since, but mine won't stop falling.

Michael took charge of the arrangements, deciding he was Margaret's family by blood and deemed it his job. *I let him.* Troy and I are a family by choice, but I don't need to be in control of the funeral arrangements.

I called Drew to let him know, but his shifts have made it hard for us to talk. I feel disconnected. "I want to come home and help you, but they won't let me take the time off. I'm so sorry, Charley," he said.

I'm so sorry. So many people have said that to me this last week I can't hear it anymore. Just leave me alone. I need to be left alone. *You need to do this first.*

I take Troy's arm, and we slowly step toward the entrance of the church. Michael's hand rubs my lower back, and I look up at him and smile. He's been a comfort these last few days, taking things off my plate and lessening the worries. I know he wants to be more intimate, but I haven't talked to Drew about him yet, so I've been holding him at arm's length. *What am I going to do about Michael?* Let's just get through the funeral first.

At the back of the church, the three of us line up behind the casket and slowly follow it inside down the center aisle. It feels stuffy, and I want to open a window. *Do the windows open?* This is Margaret's church, her community. They line the walls, standing room only. Did they all know her? How can you truly know someone? I force myself to look around and see her friends. One woman dabs her eyes with a tissue. What was her name? I glance to my right and notice Martha. *Martha is here?* Of course, she came. Just over her shoulder, I see smoky grey eyes staring at me, Drew. They must have come early to get that seat, only six pews from the front. I try to smile, but it comes out all crooked and wobbly. *He came.*

Remembering our last conversation, I turn my head and look at my feet. *Keep walking. Almost there.*

Drew wasn't happy about how Michael swooped in to help with the funeral arrangements. Our last phone call was stilted and filled with long pauses. I didn't want to call off our friends-with-benefits arrangement over the phone, but I couldn't wait any longer. *Maybe it was the wrong decision.*

"Do you want more?" I asked.

"You deserve someone like Michael," he answered. How is that an answer?

Don't I have a say in the matter? Even though Michael jumped in to help, I'm not convinced. Grief makes you do stupid things, and I refuse to do anything stupid. So, I'm on hold. Numb.

I redirected our conversation to tell him about finally finding Miss Camilla after she went missing for almost forty-eight hours. *Poor thing.* I think she knew, like she was having her last cuddles. How is it possible for a cat to know? *Don't be silly.*

My back feels hot with all the eyes on me as I take my seat in the front row between Michael and Troy. *Does Drew notice?* This is too painful. Losing Margaret and now Drew. *I miss him.* My head knows that it was time to stop our arrangement, but how it happened just sucks. I look down, linking my arm through Troy's. *Troy.* He will be my focus now.

***

The funeral is a blur, and the burial is mind-numbing. Shaking hands as people politely say their condolences. I don't remember letting go of Troy's arm, but suddenly, I realize I'm standing alone. *Where did he go?*

I scan the crowd and see he is with a group of friends. His friends came to the funeral. Oh, isn't that sweet? I want to tell Drew to look, but I remember I'm alone. Would he have wanted to be beside me? *Why does that make my heart hurt a little more?*

I keep watching Troy getting half-hugs and handshakes. He is taller than most of his friends. He's towered above me for years but seeing him with the other boys his age suddenly makes me realize how much he has grown. He must be almost six feet. *Like Nick.*

A petite girl with long brown hair stands on her tiptoes to hug him. It lasts a little too long, but maybe my sense of time is off. Is it strange how I'm just standing here watching? *Surveillance.* Yes, it's strange. *Look away.*

Then the brunette puts her arms around his shoulders, and he kisses her. Kisses her! *Oh, my god.*

Did I just witness that? I turn away. I must have been mistaken. Troy doesn't... My Troy doesn't. Does he?

Oh god, I wish I could talk to Margaret right now. She would know what to do.

I start toward the parking lot and see Michael by the limo. He is chatting with someone, but I catch his eye, and he waves me over. I scan the crowd, which has mostly dispersed, to see if maybe Drew stayed behind. I look for his truck. Nothing. Likely better we just stay apart for a bit. Maybe someday we can figure out how to be friends again.

The doubt creeps into my mind. *What makes you think that's possible after he's been in every hole?*

I approach Michael, and he opens the door for me. "Yes, that is very nice of you. Thank you. We better go now," he says to the woman as I get in the limo, and he closes the door behind me. I take a deep breath. Somehow, the tinted windows make me feel oddly safe. The other door opens and startles me. Michael, it's only Michael.

The limo driver rattles off the address to confirm our destination. "Yes, that's correct," Michael says.

"What about Troy?" I ask.

"Oh, I spoke to him earlier. He wanted to be with his friends. I didn't think you would mind," he says.

"Oh," I say, unsure if I do mind or not. Should I mind he was kissing a girl right after we buried Margaret? I close my eyes and put my head back. *So tired.*

"He is to check in with you by five o'clock. I made him promise," Michael adds.

"Thank you, I appreciate that," I say as I open my eyes and see Michael has draped his arm over the back of the seat.

"I know you are tired. Just lean on me and rest."

I don't argue. I follow the command like a good girl, unable to resist the smell of him. He wraps his arm around my shoulder, and I feel my body relax. *This is okay. It's going to be okay.* This is the man Margaret chose for me. I need to let him in... but something inside niggles as the driver abruptly rounds a corner, and we shift in our seats. I wiggle back, trying to find the spot where I can be comfortable and rest my eyes. *This isn't comfortable.* I continue to adjust, and he changes position to accommodate my fidgeting. *This is fine. No, it's not. Stay still.*

This isn't comfortable. *People can't be forced together.* Even Margaret would agree with me in the end.

We pull into Margaret's driveway, where Michael parked his car. He sends the limo driver on his way, and I am grateful that was part of the funeral arrangements. Robotically, I go to Margaret's back porch. I've been spending more time there, unable to sit in my kitchen for too long without flashbacks. Michael follows me in and asks me to sit so he can get the tea.

"There are likely some cookies up top if you like?" I call out to him. Miss Camilla jumps into my lap as soon as I have a seat. What a comfort she has been to me these last few days. We have had some interesting conversations. I can tell her anything, and she doesn't share any of my secrets.

"Are you going to come and live with me now?" I ask her. She purrs and splays her belly so I can pet her some more.

"I found some cookies; they might be a little stale, but I can get some tomorrow if you wa—" Michael doesn't finish his sentence as Miss Camilla jumps off my lap and starts hissing at him.

"Oh, my goodness, I'm so sorry!" I say, trying to control an uncontrollable cat. "I swear I never saw her do that before." Like, somehow, that makes it better. I shoo Miss Camilla out the door, and she takes off. *Damn it.* I hope she doesn't run away again. *What was that all about?*

"I've not seen her do that either. How strange," he says as he puts down the tray and pours the tea. "I have something I wanted to talk to you about."

"Oh?" I ask, hoping he won't bring up the awkwardness that happened in the limo. *Did he feel me stiffen at his touch?* Not that we have touched a lot, but it was an opportunity for us to get closer. The intimacy of going through a funeral is supposed to bond you, right? *I've watched too many rom-coms.*

"I got a new job offer, and I wanted to talk to you about it," he says.

"Oh, that's exciting."

"Yes, I will move to Cardiff," he says.

"Cardiff?" I ask.

"Yes, in Wales."

"Like overseas? Oh goodness. That's a big deal."

"Well, I debated if I should take it since things seem to be going well between us," he says.

Pardon? I try to school my face, so I don't look shocked. Maybe in his eyes, this is what that looks like? *We barely know each other!*

"I know we haven't known each other long, but I feel a chemistry between us, and I want to be with you, Charley," he says, taking my hand. I let him and gulp down my words so he can finish. *What is happening right now?*

"I was thinking you and Troy could come with me. I know this seems sudden. Hear me out," he says.

"Sudden? Michael, we barely know each other." I argue.

"We can sell both houses and make a new start in Cardiff together. I talked to the superintendent at the school board, and he said it's easy to transfer Troy. Think of the advantages he could have by finishing his diploma in another country," he says.

"But I, but... you talked to someone? About Troy?" I say. My heart races and I try to calm my thoughts to hear him out. *What is happening?*

"Yes, and I've done a bit of searching for new homes. I found this one." He takes out his phone and starts swiping to locate whatever he is looking for.

Whatever this is, it is not what I expected. *What is happening?* "I just... I can't," I say when he hands me his phone.

"Swipe left to keep going," he says, ignoring my protests. I look at the picture, and my mouth drops. Words can't explain how I can be so blindsided one moment, and so tempted the next. It's my dream home. It's a cottage with a garden and a back porch... it's... it's this house. *This house!* The house I'm in right now is just a little different, but not. He found Margarets' house in Cardiff. Wales. *Oh, my god.* Who is this man?

"I don't know what to say?" I whisper.

"Say nothing yet. I want you to think about it first. It's a big step and one I know it's making your head spin," he takes the phone from my hand and pockets it with ease. I watch his movements, noting the slight tiredness in his eyes. He has been through a lot, too.

"You should take the job," I say.

"I have time to decide. We have time," he says.

"I don't want to hold you back," I say, knowing a lump is forming in my throat. What if I'm supposed to go? *I can't go.* What if I make the wrong choice, and I mess it up all over again?

"Let's talk about it later. No rush. Can I pour the tea?"

"Yes, please," I say as we ease into the routine of teatime like we have been doing it for years. *Is this what I want?* Is this the routine I need and want?

A tear escapes and travels down my cheek. I don't want him to see my uncertainty, my hesitation, reluctance, my confusion... my sadness. I don't know what to do.

Margaret, please help me.

23

THE PATH FORWARD

DREW

I see her in the window, and for a moment, I hesitate. No, keep going. I didn't come all this way to turn around. I went to the bookstore this week only to be greeted by a sign in the window saying, 'Closed for death in the family'. Disappointed, I couldn't see her, but at least she didn't have to work this week. It's Saturday now, and I had my fingers crossed she'd be writing at the Dragonfly. Silently praying she kept up her routine. *Prayers answered.* Now what?

I get the coffees for us and have a hard time not looking over at her every five seconds. I must look like a creep or like I have a nervous tick. *I can't help it;* I'm completely drawn to this woman. She doesn't notice my obsessive checking, thank God.

Seeing her at the funeral with Michael tore my heart open. Why did I think pushing her in his direction was a good thing? I might as well have told her I didn't care. What was I thinking? *I wasn't thinking.*

I stride toward her table, and her focus is still on the screen, typing away at her keyboard. Maybe this was a bad idea.

"Anyone sitting here?" I say, putting a coffee beside her. Maybe she will see it as a peace offering. *Please don't tell me to leave.*

"Drew?" She stares up at me in disbelief.

"Me here," I say, trying to lighten the mood. She pushes her glasses up and it makes her nose squish a little. *Oh, I missed that.* I missed her.

"What are you doing here?" She asks, closing her laptop, pushing it to the side.

"I know you are writing; I apologize for interrupting you. I saw you and thought you would like a coffee. Like old times." I take a seat, noticing a little smile forming around the corners of her mouth.

"Like old times?" Her smile grows. *There it is.* She's still there. She is still Charley. The last few weeks haven't changed her... much.

"I got the keys to my new apartment today, east of downtown on Davenport Road. It's close to the highway, so I think it will be easier to get to the station." I'm rambling, not that it matters. I want to tell her all my news. I want to talk to her, my friend.

"Did your gran's house sell?" She asks.

"Yes, last week. I think the new owners are excited to move in. Not that it matters. It is just my stuff to be moved out; then, I can move on with life," I say.

"How is your Gran?" she asks.

"Driving Aunt Christine crazy, but she is good. The treatments are done, and she is stable. I don't get to see her as often with my new job," I say, casting my eyes down and taking a sip of coffee. I don't want to talk about my job; it's not been going well. Too many calls and a few too many procedural mess ups. I'm happy to have a few days off to recover.

"Well, that's good to hear." She sighs and leans back in the chair, holding her coffee to her chest on her boobie shelf. *Adorable.* Her hair is a tangled knot on her head with loose strands.

I want to fist the knot and pull her head back to expose her neck to me. My body reacts, challenging me to do it.

"I wanted to tell you again how sorry I am about Margaret," I say.

"It's okay," she sighs, the exhaustion clear in her voice. "I'm just relieved the funeral is over. That was a rough day." She pauses, and I can see the weight of everything she's been carrying, heavy on her shoulders.

I want to ask more, so many questions about how she's really feeling, but something tells me she needs a moment. So, I wait, watching the subtle shift in her expression as she gathers herself.

My patience is rewarded when her face lights up just a little, her eyes brightening as she seems to decide to let me in. "Actually, I had an appointment with a lawyer yesterday."

I straighten, instantly more alert. "Oh? Everything okay?" My voice is casual, but my gut tightens. Lawyer. It could mean a million things.

She nods, but there's hesitation there, something in the way she's choosing her words so carefully. "Yes... I mean, it's fine, but... the whole thing was unexpected."

I wait, leaning in a little, sensing there's more. She pauses, glancing down at her hand as she twists the fabric of her shirt. The silence stretches, and my mind races. *Unexpected?* What does she mean?

"I wasn't sure what to expect when I got the call," she continues. "I just... I didn't know what it was about, but I went." She shifts in her seat, clearly still unsettled by it. "Walking into the office... it felt so formal, like something out of a movie. The receptionist led me to this big conference room. I sat there alone for a few minutes, waiting." Her voice softens, and I can tell she's reliving every detail. "My heart was pounding. I kept wondering why I was even there."

Spit it out! What happened?

"The lawyer finally came in. He was this tall, older guy. Polished, serious. You know the type," she says with a faint smile. "He had this folder with him, and when he opened it, I thought my stomach was going to drop right out of my body."

I blink, hanging on her every word. "What was it about?"

She lets out a breath like she's been holding it for too long. "Margaret."

My chest tightens. "Margaret?"

She nods. "Yeah. Apparently, she left everything to me. The house, her savings... everything." She shrugs her shoulders, almost as if she's still trying to downplay it, but I can see the shock written across her face.

"Wait, everything?" I ask, my eyes wide, trying to wrap my head around the enormity of it. *Holy cow.*

She nods again, slowly, this time, letting the weight of her words settle in. "Yeah. So, I've been sitting with that. Trying to figure out what to do next."

I shake my head slightly, trying to process what she's just said. "I mean, that's... that's huge."

She lets out a shaky laugh. "Yeah, no kidding. It's like I walked in there expecting to sign a couple of papers, and I walked out with an entire life I didn't see coming."

"What are you thinking about doing?" I ask, my voice gentle, sensing that she's still overwhelmed by it all.

She sighs, rubbing the coffee cup in her hand. "I don't know. I could sell the house and move somewhere smaller. Or I could just leave town altogether. There are a lot of possibilities."

There's a long pause as she looks down at her hands, her voice softening. "But Margaret's house... it's so full of memories. It's like she's still there, you know?"

I nod, feeling the weight of her words. "Yeah. It's not just a house."

She exhales, the decision clearly weighing on her. "I just... I don't want to make the wrong choice. Margaret always said she wanted to leave me with more than just memories. I guess this is her way of doing that. But what if I screw it up?"

"You won't," I say, leaning forward. "She trusted you. She knew you'd take care of things."

Charley gives me a small, grateful smile, but I can see the uncertainty still lingering in her eyes. "Thanks. It's just... a lot to take in."

"Wow, Charley, I'm sure that's not something you expected. I'm so happy for you," I say.

"I don't know if you have time to talk about all that. I don't want to keep you." She leans forward and bites her lip. She's unsure. *Did I do that to her?* Her hesitance confirms my suspicions. I messed up, and it's time to repair the damage I've caused.

"I'm good. The rest of my day is free. I'm planning to move into the new digs tomorrow. I don't have to be back until late Wednesday."

"Well, that's a nice chunk of time to get things moved. I'm assuming you have it all arranged?" she asks.

"Yes, my buddy is helping. I'm doing it all with my truck. No need to hire anyone."

"Of course," she says, and I can't help but wonder if she would like to see the new apartment. *Maybe don't ask her today.*

"So, can I ask... about Michael?" I say. *Just dive right in.* My boldness doesn't seem to offend her as she taps her cheek with her finger.

"Michael, Michael? Sorry, do I know a Michael?" She laughs, and my heart swells at the sound. "It's been quite the adventure with him."

"Oh, yah? You care to share?" I ask. *Please tell me.* I need to know.

"Well, he took a job in Cardiff and asked Troy and I to go with him. Just this past Tuesday." She hesitates, and I try not to react, but my mouth gaps in shock. "Yup! He asked me after the funeral."

"What?" I say, unsure how her announcement can get any more shocking. "Cardiff, as in Wales?"

"Yup! And he told me he was looking at a house, which was very cute, mind you... but the next day, he came to tell me he put a down payment on it. He thought I needed to know he was serious." Her unimpressed tone helps me read between the lines. I can't imagine how Michael thought this was a good idea. My gut tightens. I need to note her reactions to this type of behavior. Maybe if I was around, he wouldn't have done that. *Too late.*

"I'm not sure I can understand how he thought that was a good idea," I say.

"Oh, he doesn't like to involve others in decisions," she says, the sarcasm dripping from her words. "By Thursday, he was on a plane."

"He left?" I say.

"Yes, he heard he wasn't named in Margaret's will, and he was quite upset. So, no more Michael," she says.

"That's a lot in three days," I add.

"I never even told Troy, not that he would have left for his senior year. Oh! And I think he has a girlfriend!" Her animated gesture at the new announcement almost hits a man trying to get past her to the restroom.

"Oh my, I'm so sorry," she says. The man shakes his head at her, and she looks at me and mouths, "Sorry".

I can't help but smile at her. This side of Charley is what I needed today. *Her. This is her.*

"I'm sorry to hear about Michael. I know Margaret really tried hard," I say.

"Drew, I know this is something that came between us, but it's all okay. I believe it happened the way it was supposed to happen. Margaret would have been so mad at him for assuming I would pick up and leave," she says as she rearranges her dress to cover her knees. I imagine what it would be like to be between them again. *Stop that.*

"You think so?" I say, trying to push away the thought of her naked in my head.

"Oh, I know so. She wanted what was best for me, not that it always made sense, but I know she wouldn't want me to become a robot and have a man make all the decisions," she says. I want to add in that she doesn't have to make all the decisions either, but how do I tell her without her taking offense?

"Drew, I know this might sound bold, but can we go back to being friends?" Her calm, serious tone makes me wonder what she is going to say next. *Can I handle being friends?*

"I really need a non-judgmental friend back in my life. You want your job back?" she asks.

"Yes," I answer without hesitation. *I want all of you, Charley.*

Her smile slowly grows, showing her teeth, and she takes off her glasses and adjusts her hair. *God, she is beautiful.*

"You know... I think Miss Camilla was trying to warn me," she says.

"What do you mean?" I ask.

"Well, she's been acting strange lately, and I know it sounds crazy, but she didn't like Michael."

"Oh?" She is right. This sounds a little crazy. It's a cat. "Maybe she is just missing Margaret?" I say.

"Well, she freaked out one day at Michael. I thought she was going to attack him. She would not calm down. I didn't know what to do."

"You think she was freaked out by Michael?" I ask.

"I think so," she says hesitantly.

"Well, maybe she's not on team Michael?"

"Definitely not. Poor thing," she says.

"Well, I'm on her team. Maybe I'll get shirts, a little one for Miss Camilla." I smile and try not to laugh as I take another sip of coffee. Charley was in the middle of a sip and almost spits it all over herself.

"Oh, my god... Can you just see that? The logo is Michael's head with a big X through it." She laughs, and I smile, basking in the moment of her lightheartedness and warmth, ecstatic now I know Michael is gone.

"The one thing about that cat is she's temperamental, but she's also agreeable company. I hate to admit how much time I'm spending at Margaret's to check on Miss Camilla. A piece of Margaret to fill in the gap."

"It's definitely a gap," I say.

She sips her coffee again; I wonder if it is almost done and if I should get another.

"It is, but I've been sorting through some things, and I'm trying to figure out the best solution," she says, pulling out a notebook from her bag.

I sit up straighter, wanting to know what she is about to tell me.

"Okay, shoot!" Charley, with a notebook, means business. I'm all in.

"Well, I was thinking I would renovate the cottage and move in," she says, opening her notebook and readying her pen.

"That's a great idea. Considering your place is now cursed," I say, hoping she might laugh at my morbid humor.

"That's what Troy said!" she says.

"See, I knew we thought alike." I wink, and she smiles at me. *My heart is melting.*

An hour later, and we have a draft plan of how to renovate the kitchen and change the flooring in the bedrooms.

"I'm hungry," hopeful she is too.

"Me too. You up to grabbing a pizza and heading to Margarets... I mean my house? I really want to measure," she says.

"Great idea. I'll get the pie and meet you there," I say, and she squeals with delight. *Her excitement is contagious.* I don't want to say anything to break the spell, though I'm tempted to apologize for being an ass these last few weeks.

"I'll see you in a bit!" She goes up on her tiptoes and pecks my cheek.

It's just a friendly gesture. *Don't overthink it.* She gets her things and rushes out.

I slow my stride behind her to watch how she bobs up and down as she heads for her car. *How is she so frigg'n adorable?* How am I going to get out of the friend zone? I sigh, trying to reassure myself. If this is what our relationship will be, then so be it. Better than no Charley. *Who am I kidding?* I want more. I need more.

CHARLEY

Troy isn't home when I arrive, so I dump my bag with my laptop in the kitchen and start looking in the junk drawer for a measuring tape. Notebook in hand, I head over to Margarets'. *Do I keep calling it that?* Maybe it's Miss Camilla's house now.

She greets me at the door like she can hear my thoughts. I reach down, and she lets me hold her close as I scratch her ears. "Did you have a good day? Oh good.

Well, Drew is coming over, so I hope you don't mind." I tell her.

"Mom?" Troy opens the door and steps inside. "Who are you talking to? The cat?"

"Yes, I am," I say in a singsong voice. "She seems to like it." Miss Camilla's purring gets louder as she pushes her head into my neck.

"Guess so. Can I have Thomas over?" he asks.

"Yes, I'm here for a bit. Drew is coming over. You remember Drew?"

"Yah," he hesitates a little before scrolling through his phone.

I hear the hesitation, the uncertainty. It lingers in the space between my thoughts, and I feel the weight of it pressing down on me. Miss Camilla jumps from my lap.

I glance over at Troy, busy with whatever has captured his attention, completely unaware of the storm brewing inside me. I don't want to force Drew and Troy together today. It's too soon for that. But I'm tired of hiding. Tired of pretending this is enough for me.

The friends-with-benefits arrangement has run its course. I thought it would be easy, as if keeping things casual would protect me. But it's left me feeling empty.

I want more, something real. Something Drew may not even be willing to give. That's the part making my chest tighten. I don't know how he feels. I don't know if I'm about to risk everything by wanting more.

I steal another glance at Troy, grateful he's too distracted to notice the turmoil in my eyes. He doesn't need to know his mom is tangled in something she's not sure how to handle.

But I can't keep doing this. The thought is firm, and the realization hits me like a wave. I've been holding back, staying in the shadows, afraid of what might happen if I ask for more. But I can't live in this half-life anymore, pretending a casual relationship is enough when I know it's not.

I feel the fear creeping in, the what ifs, the doubts. What if Drew doesn't feel the same? What if he's perfectly content with what we have, and asking for more pushes him away? But underneath my fear, there's a quiet strength building. I'm ready to step into the light, to stop hiding how I feel.

Troy doesn't need to know this battle is happening. But I know it's time. It's time to take a risk, even if I don't know how Drew will respond.

"Well, Drew agrees this place needs a new kitchen. He likes my idea, and he's coming to do some measuring and planning with me. Oh, and he's bringing pizza," I say in Troy's direction, unsure if he's even listening.

"Pizza? Can I have some?" he asks. *I guess he was listening.*

"Of course." I laugh, wondering if I should text Drew to get a large. "I know we talked a bit about the idea of fixing this place and selling it, but what if we moved in here instead?" I say to Troy.

Troy knows about the will. I've been open with him about my meeting with the lawyer. We had a family meeting and I'm so proud of how he has handled all these changes in our life. *He's growing up.* It's time for me to give him the respect of having a say in our family matters. I am grateful I don't have to do it alone.

"I was thinking the same thing. I don't want to live in the cursed house anymore. Let's live with Miss Camilla," he says.

"Deal." But before I can get my hand out to shake his, he's out the door. "Where are you going?" I call out.

"To pack!" he yells back. I shake my head; I expected a yes, but not so fast.

Drew arrives, and we spend over an hour measuring and taking notes between bites of pizza. I'm excited with his idea of how to open the space but preserve the 1940s architecture.

"I'm tempted to get a crowbar!" I say.

"I know you are, but a few more weeks and you can move in," he reassures.

"I got it!" A voice from the back door yells, and Troy waddles in, holding two garbage bags and a duffle bag slung over his shoulder.

"Hi, Drew," Troy says as Thomas comes up behind him, holding Troy's nightstand.

"What's going on?" I say, hands on my hips, glaring at my son.

"This is Thomas. Thomas, you know my mom. This is Drew," Troy says. Even though I'm happy he remembered his manners, I still want him to answer my question.

"Hi Thomas, would you boys like some pizza?" Drew says, offering one of the three boxes. He had arrived with three medium pizzas because he didn't know what toppings I wanted. I know it was too much, but deep down I was happy there was plenty for tonight and for leftovers tomorrow.

The boys drop everything they are carrying and dive into the pizza. I count in my head. *Calm down.* Trust he will tell you what is happening in a moment.

"You helpin' with the kitchen?" Troy asks Drew.

My arms drop to my sides. Well, this is new.

"Yes, your mom has some good ideas. Want to know what we've got planned?" Drew looks up at me and winks.

Troy says an enthusiastic yes through a mouthful of meat-lovers pizza. I knew he'd want that one. It's why I went for the pepperoni and cheese.

"That's cool!" Thomas chimes in as Drew explains the drawing from my notebook.

"Are we doing the front bedroom?" I think Troy is asking Drew, but he is looking at me.

"Well, maybe just take out the carpet, but nothing major," Drew answers for me.

"Why?" I ask.

"Cuz, I'm claiming it," Troy says.

"You are claiming it? What does that mean?" I ask.

"It means I'm moving into that room. It's a suitable spot for me and you can have all upstairs to yourself," he says as he grabs a second slice. How does he inhale that so fast?

"That's fine. Is that what all of this is about?" I say, gesturing to the bags now littering the kitchen.

"Yes, I'm not staying another night in the cursed house. I want to move in now."

My eyes widen, and I notice Drew gesturing at me.

"I agree, it's cursed," Drew says.

"See! Drew agrees with me," Troy says as if it will help his argument.

How did I get in the middle of this one? How did my world get turned upside down but feel so right?

"Fine," I cave. "You can sleep here tonight. There is a bed in there already. We can move your bed tomorrow if you want, but not tonight."

"Woohoo!" Troy high fives Thomas.

"See, told ya, dude, if you showed up with your stuff, she would say yes," Thomas chimes in.

I shake my head and close my eyes. *This is my new life.* I feel something at my ankle, and Miss Camilla is making a figure eight as she walks between my legs. *Yes, my sweet girl, I agree; it's going to be a good life.*

24

ROCK, PAPER, SCISSORS

CHARLEY

It's Sunday morning, and I decide not to go to church. "I know Margaret will be upset with my decision," I tell Miss Camilla as I continue to pack boxes and fill the living room with kitchen items.

I couldn't sleep last night. A mix of excitement about making Margaret's house our new home and nervous because Troy stayed alone in the new house. *Stubborn.* I am not ready to make the change until the renovations are done, cursed house or not. It's still my house.

The top cupboards are empty, and I've made three piles: keep, donate, garbage. I glance at my phone and notice 11:11. Church service has started. *Push away the guilt.* It's not like I haven't missed church before, but I'm not sure how I fit without Margaret there.

"I should go put some flowers on her grave this week," I say to Miss Camilla, who is sunbathing in the window. Ahh, a cat's life, having to listen to the mutterings of their humans.

Everything is now in the apartment. Didn't take too long.

That's great.

I'm going to put the new bedframe together, so I don't have to sleep on the floor. How is the packing going at your end?

Very well. She had a lot of things, but I am only keeping what I think I need.

She must have entertained the neighbourhood at one point, lol

Ha!

Want to come over for a bit to eat later? You can see the new place, and we can order from the new Thai place?

Sounds like a great idea. I'm in.

Perfect. 6?

6ish? Send me the address.

I put down my phone. It's too tempting to continue distracting myself with this conversation. I grab another box and start on the lower cabinets, promising myself I will stop with enough time to get cleaned up before seeing Drew.

I turn on the radio, letting the soft hum of music keep me company as my thoughts wander to what my new house will look like once I'm finished. *My house.* It still feels strange to say it, to think of this space as mine. *Thank you, Margaret.*

Miss Camilla lets out a loud meow, her voice breaking through my thoughts. I smile, glancing over as she jumps off the windowsill. "Oh, you want to thank her too?" I tease as she trots toward me, her steps almost playful.

She leaps into my lap as I sit on the floor, a colander in one hand and a mixing bowl in the other. "What is this?" I ask, surprised by her sudden burst of affection. She purrs, her soft fur brushing against my chest and neck, her head nudging me with a warmth I didn't know I needed.

I stroke her, feeling a wave of emotion building inside me. "Thank you, Miss Camilla. And thank you, Margaret." The words come out quieter this time, my heart swelling with gratitude as it all sinks in. Margaret gave me more than just a house—she gave me a future, a place where I could start again.

As Miss Camilla's purring fills the room, my thoughts drift back to Margaret, and for a moment, I'm overwhelmed by how much she meant to me. She wasn't just a friend; she was a steady presence, the one person who seemed to always know what I needed, even when I didn't. We spent so many afternoons together, drinking tea in her sunroom, sharing stories, sometimes in silence, but always comfortable; we didn't need words to feel understood.

Margaret taught me how to find strength in the quiet moments, how to appreciate the simple things, like the way sunlight filters through the trees, or the satisfaction of blooms that come back the following year. She was there for me when I thought I had no one. And now, even though she's gone, she's still giving me a sense of stability. I feel it in this house, in the rooms she inhabited and the memories she left behind.

But as the gratitude washes through me, it's tinged with the sadness of loss. She's not here anymore. I won't hear her laugh or see the way her eyes crinkled when she teased me. I won't get to thank her in person for all she did. But I can feel her presence, almost like she's still watching over me, nudging me forward, reminding me I'm not alone.

Miss Camilla shifts in my lap, her warmth grounding me in the present. I take a deep breath, letting the emotion flow through me, and for the first time in a long while, I feel like I'm ready to move forward. The grief is still there, but it's softer now, a gentle reminder of the love we shared.

"Thank you, Margaret," I whisper again, the words less heavy this time, more like a quiet goodbye.

***

I knock on the door marked 305 at five after six. Finding the place didn't take me too long, but I waited in my car until six o'clock, not wanting to seem too eager. *Why am I so nervous?*

It will be my first time alone with him in what feels like forever, and I just don't know what to expect. The old feelings are still there, but maybe he just wants to be friends. Do friends do these kinds of things? *I should just tell him.*

Confession time! Drew, I want more than a fuck buddy. I want a relationship. *I want us.* And I want to see if we can make this work. The thought alone sends a thrill through me, my pulse quickening as my imagination runs wild. I've been practicing what I'll say all afternoon, but my mind keeps wandering, replaying every moment with Drew. His smile, his laugh, the way his hand feels on mine. It's all so effortless with him, so *natural.*

But what if he doesn't see it that way? What if he doesn't want more? The thought makes my stomach flip. *What if he does?*

A rush of excitement floods through me. The possibility of something real, something lasting, sends my heart racing. I bite my lip, feeling the buzz of anticipation build inside me. This could be the start of something big—or the moment everything changes.

Drew opens the door and greets me with a big smile, putting me at ease. "Welcome to my humble abode," he says.

"Wow, nice spot." I take in the open concept and see he has a balcony overlooking a park. It's impressive. Just the basics for furniture, but what he has is arranged tastefully.

"I met my neighbour, and he seems nice. Older gentleman," he offers.

I admit I immediately thought about a young woman who would introduce herself, and my jealousy volume turned up. *What was that about?*

"That's nice. You seem to have things all set up," I say.

"Well, I don't have much, so it didn't take long," he says.

"Here, I got you this." I hand him a bag. "Sorry, I didn't wrap it."

"Champagne?" He hugs me and says thank you into my hair. I feel my body relax into him. I want to minimize the gift, but his reaction is so overwhelmingly welcome, I don't say a word.

"Let's order the food?" He pulls out of the hug. "I have the menu right here." Looking it over, my mouth waters. Each item has a picture featuring deliciousness.

"That! I want that!" I say, pointing. He already has his phone out to make the call.

"Very decisive," he says.

"I know what I like," I say as I look at him in his tight grey t-shirt, which highlights the muscles of his chest and arms. *I like that.* I fight the urge to add how much I want to eat him up.

"Hi, I would like to place an order for delivery," he says into the phone.

I walk toward the patio door and admire the view. Even from the third floor, he is high enough to enjoy the lushness of the trees in the park. The street below has the occasional car. I can see mine is exactly where I left it. No ticket, I note.

"Yes. Thank you. Okay." Drew hangs up. "The food will be here in twenty minutes."

"Perfect, I'm starving," I say.

"I'll get some glasses," he says.

I grab the champagne and head for the couch. Even though I have only been in his apartment for ten minutes, something inside me shifts as he comes toward me. *Something feels different.* Excitement fills my chest as my heart seems to stretch in his direction. *What is happening?*

He doesn't say a word; just takes the champagne and opens it like a pro. POP!

"Woohoo! You didn't spill a drop." I smile.

"Thank you," he says as he pours. "Thank you for celebrating my first night here."

"It's a great spot. I'm so happy you finally found a place, and your gran's house is sold. I can't imagine what it was like to pack up over fifty years of memories."

"Did I tell you about how I found a box of old letters?" he says.

"No!" I say, excited to hear the story. His animated story-telling puts me at ease, and I sit back and realize how relaxed I am. It must be the champagne. *No, it's him. It's always been him.* I add in my questions, not thinking through my words before they come out of my mouth. I am not shy or, embarrassed or worried about saying the wrong thing. I'm just me... and I feel alive. Our conversation shifts to the kitchen renos, and he says he can come tomorrow to help me clear out the garbage.

"As long as you wear your hat backwards," I laugh.

"You like that?" he asks as he tops up my drink.

I want to touch him so badly, but I just smile and nod. A buzzer goes off, and I jump at the noise. "Our food is here," he says.

"I'll get some plates," I say, moving to the kitchen in hopes it will be easy to find what I need. We put everything out to examine our choices. "It smells amazing," I say, dishing up.

"Did you sort the kitchen stuff you want to keep? No table settings for twelve?" he asks. We ease back into conversation, and I tell him about the interesting items I found.

"Honestly, I thought you might bring stuff here," he says.

"You need a salad spinner? She had three," I say.

"Of course! Doesn't every new home need three salad spinners?" I almost choke on my pad Thai noodles.

"Oh, sorry. You, okay? I didn't mean to make you laugh with a mouth full of food."

"It's okay... water?" I cough and try to catch my breath. "I should know better than to eat with Mr. Funnyman." I tease.

He hands me a glass of water, and I drink. "Better?"

"Yes, thank you," I say.

He puts his hand on my back and rubs. "Sorry."

"I'm okay. No worries," I say realizing the coughing has stopped, but now I'm holding my breath. *He's so close.* He doesn't stop touching me as I turn toward him. The air is electric. His hand moves toward my face, and time slows.

His mouth is on mine, and I don't stop him. How can I stop him? *I want this.* I need this.

Hooking my hands behind his back, I lean into his kiss like a teenager with raging hormones. His tongue sweeps into my mouth, and he tastes like supper. *I must taste the same.*

Our mouths never stop touching, as our hands explore each other. Even though we have done this before, somehow, it just feels different. I can't get enough of him. I'm hungry for more.

"'Charley,' he breathes. The sound of my name on his lips ignites a flame inside me, and I feel the stir of desire awakening within me."

"Wait," he says, pulling me away from him.

Wait? Wait what? I ignore him, unable to get enough of his tongue. I sigh and press myself into him, and feeling his solid strength makes me want to get lost in this moment.

He puts his hand up my shirt, and I feel his thumb rub my nipple; only the thin barrier of fabric of my bra between us, but it responds all the same. The way his hands feel on me and his mouth feels on mine, I am unraveling the stories I've been creating in my mind. The stories of Michael... Nick... no one has ever touched me like this.

He is erasing them, blowing them to dust and replacing them with only him. *How is he doing this to me?*

He takes my hand, leading me to the living room. I know he wants to undress me, and I desperately want to undress him, but something in his posture has me hesitating.

"I want you, Charley," he says.

I take a sharp inhale, startled by the way he is looking at me.

"I don't want to go back to the arrangement we had. I want more."

"More?" I ask. My mind is spinning. *What is he going to say next?*

"Yes, so if you don't want that... well, we can stop. I can stop," he says.

I can't.

"Drew, would you like to negotiate?" I tease, knowing it worked the first time, so why wouldn't it now?

"Yes, that is exactly what I want," he says.

"Perfect. You go first." I say, moving back to the stool and away from him. I don't trust myself to touch him during this conversation.

"Yes. First rule. I need you to be honest and direct. I will give it, and I expect it back," he says.

I nod in agreement. *That is a great rule.*

"I understand. Second rule. We are not a secret. We need to tell Troy," I say, crossing my arms across my chest, wondering if he'll see this as a deal breaker.

"Second rule... amendment," he says. I cock an eyebrow at him. "I want to tell Troy. You can be there, but I want him to hear it from me."

Well, that was a surprise. My stance softens, and I lick my lips.

"Deal," I confirm.

"Third rule. We set up a way to stay in contact when I'm at the station. I don't want you worried about me or thinking you can't get me if you need me. I have a few ideas on how to do that, and we can figure out the logistics later," he says.

"Okay, I agree. Thank you for thinking about that issue. It was hard when we didn't have contact." I swallow at the memory.

"I know, I'm sorry. It will be better. We'll figure it out together," he says, reaching out to touch me.

I hold up a hand. "Don't touch me yet, or I won't be able to get this out," I say.

"Sorry, go ahead."

"My last rule is when there is something bothering me, or I feel uncertain about, I want to say one word, and you will know. We don't have to talk about it right at that moment, but it's like a way to communicate quickly."

"So, like an emotional safe word?" he asks.

"Yes." Oh, he is catching on faster than I thought. "How about... pumpernickel."

"Sounds perfect," he laughs as he repeats the safe word, dragging every syllable.

"Meeting adjourned?" I ask.

"Yes. Thank you for telling me what you need. I want that. Always." He moves toward me again, but I move backward slightly, knowing that if I don't get this part out before he touches me, I won't.

"Drew, this is really helpful for me, but I feel like I'm going to explode if you touch me right now. I hate to admit how much I want to rip off your clothes," I say.

"Honest and direct. I love it." He winks at me, and I purse my lips together, so my laugh comes out my nose.

I admit I'm a little nervous to be completely naked in this half-lit room. *Why am I nervous?* This man has seen every inch of me! But this time just feels different. Like I've crossed a boundary. *We've crossed it together.* Thank god we are on the other side. I walk into the living room and wonder if I should just strip or let him take off my clothes.

I turn to face him, trying to read his thoughts, when I see a devilish smile form.

"Rock, paper, scissors?" he asks.

"Perfect." I smile.

"Socks count as one piece of clothing," he announces. I laugh again and look down. I don't have socks, but he does. How is that a good rule for him? I count the pieces of clothing I have on, four. Shit. I'll be naked in no time.

"1-2-3 shoot," he shouts, and I win with rock.

I creep toward him and grab the hem of his shirt, slowly peeling it off him and inhaling his scent. Oh, I missed that. What a sight. I toss his shirt on the couch, and we start again.

"1-2-3 shoot!" I shout, and he wins with paper. He isn't as gentle as I feel my shirt up over my head. Hair falling in my face. *Where did my elastic go?*

"1-2-3 shoot!" he shouts, and I win. I point at his socks.

"Off," I command. I win two more times, and I'm giddy at the thought of my streak as I look to see I'm still only missing my shirt. I laugh as he stands before me in only his boxers.

"I'm winning!" I say, clapping my hands and jumping childishly. *Am I really winning if he's naked, and we are standing here with only one shirt off?*

He puts his hands on his hips and laughs. "I'm losing this game."

"I think I'm losing," I say, gesturing to my current dressed state.

"Nah," he says. "You win." He comes toward me, takes my face in his hands, and puts his mouth on mine.

The humor is gone as his lips trail down my neck, and he slowly undresses me. He takes his time to unbutton, unhook and drag the fabric over my skin. Kissing me in its wake.

Game over.

He backs away to gaze at me and takes off his boxers without breaking eye contact.

I am exposed... vulnerable... seen.

We stand looking at each other. The moment seems frozen in time. I drink him in. The way he is comfortable in his skin makes me comfortable too. I am on display for him and as his breath quickens, a hunger seems to rumble within him that makes me ache to be touched.

He leads me to the kitchen island, pushing our leftovers out of the way.

I am unsure what he is doing, but the overwhelming heat between my legs makes me eager to please. *Follow his lead.*

"Lay down. I want dessert," he says, grabbing me around the waist to lift me up on the island. *Holy shit.*

The hardness against my back and hips reminds me this is real. I'm not imagining this from my bedroom with a vibrator inside me. The dim lights shine down on me, and I realize there is nowhere to hide. My legs are bent, knees tight together. *I'm nervous.* Why am I so nervous?

I hold the edge of the countertop to steady myself. I will not fall. He won't let me fall. *I am safe.*

"Let me see Charley," he says in a voice that makes my insides relax. My legs part, and he takes my thighs to open them wider. *He wants to see, let him.*

"Such a good girl to listen so well," he purrs.

Did he just call me a good girl? Oh god, how did that just turn up my dial so high? Am I this wet? I moan.

His hands rub my thighs and up to my hips, grabbing my behind to meet his mouth. He just dove in! Licking and sucking, and oh my god, I'm going to lose it. My nails dig into the counter, and I squirm.

He lets me go, and my legs open for him, wanting that sweet release.

"Oh god!" I scream. His mouth sucks, and his chin is buried so I can feel the gentle rasp of his scruff. I want to rub into him, knowing I need the sensation to pull me over the edge. My back arches as my legs shake.

His enthusiasm intensifies as he grabs my wrists to steady me and pull me closer.

My back bows more, knowing I'm off the hard surface, as my head rocks back to hold me more in place. I hear the slurps like he is drinking from a fountain to quench his thirst. I push my heels onto the table to steady myself as my orgasm hits me like a freight train.

"Oh my god!" I scream again as my chest rises higher, almost like it can touch the light above me. I'm exploding from the inside. This must be what oblivion feels like.

My body relaxes, and my legs tremor with aftershocks.

He moves to help me sit up and pulls me into his arms, cradling me as he moves me to the couch. I melt into him. *What the hell was that?*

DREW

She's a little shaky, so I hold her for a while. Rocking her in my arms. I've not seen that intensity from her before. *Her body responds to me. Period.* I've never had another woman who showed me that before, but Charley lets go. I'm familiar with her letting go and trusting me with her body, but tonight was different. What just happened is all new.

Her back arched so much I thought she was going to bend in half. I couldn't stop... eating. It's like I was possessed. I needed to feel her throb in my mouth and taste her juices. I can't get enough. When I finally stopped, I saw the way the light shone down on her skin. Like she was on stage, a spotlight highlighting her essence. Rapidly blinking to see if the image changed, how could that be real? *That's what she needs. She needs to be in the spotlight. I need to help her shine.*

I lay her down, check she is okay and grab her a blanket. I'm not sure if she sees how hard I am for her, but I refuse to cover up my nakedness or excuse the throbbing in my core. I know I will have a release soon.

I wrap her up and kneel beside her. My gentle rubbing of her arm and back seems to ease her breath. She is coming back to reality. My breath matches hers, and her eyes flutter open, examining my face. *She's so beautiful it makes me ache.*

"I love you. I've known that for a long time and wanted to say it out loud." She closes her eyes after it comes out of her mouth. Her words take me unaware. *What? How? When?* But just like that... The next piece of the puzzle just clicks into place.

25

PLAYER OF THE YEAR

Two weeks later

CHARLEY

Drew parks the truck at the far end of the ball diamond. The parking lot is full, and we have a hard time finding a spot. "Hurry! They already started," Drew says as I pull the hoodie over my head.

"I'm coming!" I say as I notice he appears beside me to open the passenger door of the truck.

"No, that was an hour ago, and why we are late," he says, holding out a hand to help me down and planting a kiss on my lips. *Best part about not being a secret, PDA.* He shuts the door with his other hand, refusing to let go of mine.

"All good?" he asks. I look down at the dolphin logo and smile.

"All good, he's going to be so embarrassed," I say.

Troy might not like the official Dolphin's logo, but when I told Drew the story, he thought it would be nice to have matching hoodies made for his last regular game of the year. The front is the cartoon dolphin with the ball on its nose, cute. And we added 'Go Troy Go' on the back. I can't wait to see his reaction.

As we go toward the bleachers, I see there aren't many other people watching. Not that I mind. Plenty of places to sit, I guess.

Drew takes the first step up and turns to help me. You would think I never climbed bleachers on my own before, the way he is so attentive.

"I can manage," I say as my foot moves to the next step; my toe catches the edge, and I face plant into him. *Well, damn.*

"I know you can," he laughs as he helps me find my footing and I sit on the second-row bench, refusing to go any further. I don't trust my feet at this point.

"This is where you want to sit?" he asks.

"No, but it's fine." I shake my head at my klutziness. "We don't want to be too close to the dugout and embarrass Troy... yet."

He smiles and squeezes my hand. "God, I love you."

"Love you too." I plant a kiss on his cheek. *I will never tire of that.*

We watch as the Dolphins take the field, and I take my hand out of his so I can clap. It might be their last game of the season. If they don't win, they don't make the finals. I can see Troy shaking out his shoulders as he heads to first base and flexes his glove. I tried to give him a pep talk about today's game, but he told me I was embarrassing myself.

'Stop, please stop, Mom,' is Troy's mantra lately. I come to all the games. I'm familiar with the players, but I admit, sometimes it's so boring, and I scroll on my phone. Oh well, I pay attention when it matters.

His coach called to tell me he made Player of the Year for the Dolphins. He wanted to give me a heads-up so I could have my camera ready today. Camera. *Do I own a camera anymore?* My phone will have to do.

"Troy doesn't know, so don't say anything," Coach said.

I didn't. Well, I told Drew, but that doesn't really count. Drew had the matching shirts made, and I love him a little more for wanting to make today fun. *Well, fun for us.*

I hear the crack of the bat and look up to see Troy waiting to receive the ball from his outfielder. "OUT!" I cheer as I see the hand signal of the umpire.

"Way to go Troy!" Drew calls out with his hands, cupping his mouth to project the sound. I smile at his enthusiasm. Ever since we had our chat with Troy about our new dating status, things have been easier between them. Drew was open about his expectations and gave Troy time to process.

Troy's initial reaction was a little cool, but he's slowly warming to our new arrangement. Some days, I watch them move around each other like wolves deciding who is alpha... men, ugh. Other times, they get into deep conversations about where Troy will go to college.

I have learned more about Troy's inner thoughts about eavesdropping this last month than I have in years. *Interesting, very interesting.*

Another ball hit, and it bounces along the ground. The pitcher picks it up and tosses it to Drew. Another out, but I refrain from yelling commentary this time.

"He's playing well today. Looks like he's shaking off the nerves," Drew says as he puts his hand around my back and gives me a little squeeze.

"Go, Troy, Go." I look up and smile at Drew.

"I never asked you much about Nick. I know he played ball, but was he any good?" Drew asks, and I startle at the question.

"Umm, yes. I guess. You don't know what happened to Nick?" I ask.

"Not really. Just that he left. Gran told me he *chose baseball over family,* but I didn't really think much about it until now," Drew says.

"Yes. Do you want to know more?" I ask, concerned that this might not be the best place to have this conversation.

He seems to catch my meaning and squeezes my shoulder again. "Maybe later."

I nod and look down at our matching shirts now side my side. The logos are the same size, but mine fills the entire front of my chest. His looks more normal on his front and doesn't pop out like mine, making it look like I'm a snowball.

"You look adorable," he says.

Damn it, he read my mind again.

I smile, knowing Troy might die of embarrassment. I can't wait to see his reaction.

The next few innings creep by with little excitement. No one seems to hit or get on base. Then Troy steps to the plate.

"Let's go, Troy!" I shout, and Drew claps along with me. "Please, please, please," I pray to the sky and cross my fingers.

The ball leaves the pitcher's hand, and before I can register the movement and sound, Troy is running for first base. The outfielder misses, and Troy is now running for second base. Drew and I are on our feet screaming!

The play finishes and we slowly find our seats again, but not before I notice a petite brunette standing off to our left, bouncing up and down, clapping. *That must be her.*

Excitement fills me at the thought of knowing the new girlfriend is here. Should we go say hi? Do I wait until the end of the game? What is the etiquette?

"I think that's the new girlfriend," I say into Drew's ear.

"Huh? What? Where?"

"Not so loud," I say. Ugh! "Just be subtle. She is standing beside the stands to your right. Brunette. You can barely see the top of her head right now."

I see his eyes track, and he follows my instructions. "Yah, 100%. That looks like Jamie," he says, turning back to me.

"Jamie?" I say.

"Not so loud!" he says, smirking at me.

"Okay, you got me. Please tell me how you know her name," I ask.

"I asked him. I thought you knew. I would have told you. Sorry," he says, shrugging.

I grab and squeeze his knee in frustration, knowing my grip strength will not put much pressure.

"No, I did NOT know. Tell me these things," I whine. Whining? *Is that what we are doing now?*

"I'm sorry, Baby girl, I thought you knew," he looks at me in surprise. "Well, the new girl is Jamie. Remember, you thought he was with someone at the funeral? You were right. That looks like her. He showed me a picture and told me her name was Jamie," he says.

I give a back-handed slap and hit him in the chest.

"Ouch!"

"Oh, as if that hurt. No, I did not know. He showed you a picture?"

"STRIKE!" I hear the umpire interrupting my moment of confusion and replacing it with what is happening on the diamond. *Where is Troy?* I scan and see he's still on second base, posed to take off at the next hit.

"I'm sorry. I thought you knew. I was just making small talk a few days ago, and he wouldn't shut up about her."

I glare at him. What the heck is going on? Why am I not in the loop? I huff a breath, and he grabs me close.

"I promise to tell you all about it, and I promise I will tell you everything from now on."

"STRIKE!" I see Troy shifting, but I focus on Drew's words in my ear.

"I promise to make it up to you. Can you forgive my assumptions?" I nod at his words. The crack of the bat stops our semi-embrace, and I jump to my feet.

"Go, Troy!" I scream and clap as I see him running for third and being signaled to run toward home. I glance at the brunette, Jamie, who is now jumping up and down, screaming his name. Torn between jealousy of not being part of this new relationship and pride for him to have found someone who seems so excited. *She has nice hair.* Her long, dark locks sway as she jumps.

I glance back to the game just in time to see Troy slide home. The ball tags him too late. I yip and yell, embarrassing myself by jumping like Jamie. Her energy is contagious.

Drew stands beside me, clapping hard and screaming. "Atta boy, Troy!"

My chest swells at the thought of how Drew and Troy seem to have bonded a little over their Jamie talk. Maybe it's not so bad after all. I look and see Troy giving a wave to Jamie, acknowledging her praise. He looks toward the bleachers and catches my eye. I frantically wave at him and blow him two handed kisses with full arm movements like I did when he was young. He shakes his head, and I laugh. Then he does a double take.

"You see him?" I say.

"Yup," Drew says, continuing to clap.

Troy leans over and squints a little in our direction. "He's trying to see the shirts. Wanna turn around?"

"Yup! Ready? 1-2-3." I yell, trying to keep eye contact with Troy. Drew turns gracefully, and I shuffle around, concerned I will fall off the small perch for our feet. He takes my hand and throws up our arms into the air. My other arm follows suit, and we yell in unison.

"Go, Troy, Go!"

I look at Drew and laugh. The other people in the stands are looking at us. A few chuckles and one man laughing hysterically.

"I wish I thought about doing that!" he says to us as we lower our arms and turn around.

I see Troy is walking back to the dugout, shaking his head. *Mission accomplished.*

I start to sit and see Jamie is looking in our direction. I smile at her, and she smiles back. A sweet smile that I try to reflect. *Oh, please don't break my son's heart.*

"Maybe we can meet her after the game?" Drew says as he notices the smile interaction.

"Maybe," I say.

The next few innings have some near misses that make the crowd grumble and grow impatient. We are down six runs; the game is basically over, and we are just waiting for the last inning to play out. No playoffs in sight this year.

I try to watch Troy, but I'm restless in my seat. I want to meet Jamie and how am I going to make that happen? I run options in my mind, thinking of how to make it natural. It's not like I can bump into her and introduce myself.

Troy will be mortified if I embarrass him further. A cartoon dolphin on a hoodie is one thing. Awkward mother-girlfriend meeting is another.

"Don't overthink it. I can hear the wheels turning in your head," Drew says beside me.

"I know, sorry."

"What can I do to get you to relax?" he says.

"Umm, well, nothing here," I say, looking ahead and trying my best not to meet his eyes.

"You want to come to my place after the game, then? I have a few ideas on how to clear that head of yours," he offers.

"Do tell," I challenge, wondering if he will be bold enough to say it to me here with so many people around.

"I want to tie you to my bed and have my way with you. Lick you until you beg for me to be inside you, and then deny you just a little longer," he says into my neck.

"Oh my," I close my eyes and try to stop the sounds from leaving my mouth. He turns back to look at me.

"Open your eyes. Can't let the people around know what we are talking about. Try to focus on the game, Charley." He slips his arm over my shoulder, and his finger brushes my neck.

I swallow. "That's impossible. You better stop," I say.

"Not impossible. You like challenges." He teases and strokes the curve of my ear, rubbing the lobe. *How is that turning me on right now?*

The last batter throws his bat, and then his helmet in anger. I see the players coming in off the field, signaling the end of the game. We stand and start clapping.

Drew winks at me, and I remind myself how much he can make my body sing his song.

The winning team coach calls his players to home plate to do his pep talk. I look for our team and notice they are moving off the field to a bench near the parking lot. The usual spot he takes them to post-game. The fans move closer but don't want to interrupt the coach's pep talk. To our surprise, he calls us all over to join him. We are a group of about twenty and I scan for Jamie. *Where is she?*

"This has been an exceptional year for our team. I know it didn't end the way we hoped, but it was..." the coach's voice continues to drone on, but I am not paying attention.

Drew is behind me and grabs my hand, pulling me a little closer so I can feel the solidness of him behind me.

"I'm going to make you cum so hard tonight, you are going to wake the neighbours," he says into the back of my neck.

I have a hard time keeping a straight face. I focus on the man in front of me with his meaty ankles stuffed into white socks and sneakers that have seen better days. I squirm a little, and Drew releases me to clap. I follow his lead. If he's clapping, then I should clap. I look around and see others are doing the same. *What are we clapping for?* I need to talk to him about how he flips that switch inside me.

I look to my left and see small hands attached to petite arms, also clapping. I follow them up and see they belong to Jamie. *She is right there.* Do I say something?

I feel a hand come down on my shoulder. Drew's reassuring hand reminds me he is close. "Hi, I'm Drew, and this is Charley," he says, holding out a hand. We form a little awkward triangle and shake each other's hands. Jamie doesn't offer her name. Just a meek hello, and her cheeks flush.

"I like your sweaters. Troy might not see the humor, but someday he will," Jamie says.

"Thank you," I say. *Oh, I like her already.*

"And player of the year is... Troy Thomas!" The coach announces, and everyone bursts into applause. "We are past medals and trophies here, so this is what we got you instead." He hands him a t-shirt. Troy barely looks at it before his head looks at the sky, and he mutters.

"What does it say?" Drew yells at him, trying to make it sound like he is an unknown fan in the crowd.

Troy shakes his head and turns the shirt around, holding it up against his uniform. It's clear as day, and I can't stop laughing at his embarrassment. It's the Dolphins logo, same as the one on mine and Drew's hoodies, with 'Player of the Year' stencilled across the top. *I'm loving this.*

"We match!" I yell, pulling the logo on my shirt and helping Drew to come beside me and mimic me.

Troy puts his face in his hands and balls up the shirt. He puts out his hand and thanks his coach. *Good boy.*

"Hey, can I get one of those?" I hear a voice from my right. "Ya! I want one too."

"Sure, I can get you one. They are one of a kind," I say, smiling. What have I done? I've made this joke a popular fashion item.

"You take the orders; I'll get them made," Drew says to me.

I mouth a thank you, grateful he knows I don't want to be managing the impulse purchases from so many people. I go on my tiptoes and plant a quick kiss on his lips.

"Gross." I turn and see Troy beside me, holding Jamie's hand. She has her other hand on his biceps, leaning into him slightly.

"Hello, Mr. Player," I tease.

"Congratulations Troy," Drew says, holding out his hand to shake Drews free one.

"Thanks. I need some food," Troy says, making sure we all know his stomach needs are paramount.

"Sure, you want to all go out for pizza?" I say, but as the words leave my mouth, I know it was a mistake by the look on Troy's face.

Drew saves me and reaches for his wallet. "Here is some money. How about you two head out for food? I leave in the morning and would like to take your mom out alone. Is that okay with you?" Drew says to Troy. *He asked Troy.* He didn't ask me, I note. Not that it matters.

"Ya, sounds good. See you at home later Mom." He comes in to hug me and I hold him in my arms, pride sticking in my throat so much I fight the tears. Since Margaret passed, he has become a hugger. *I'm not complaining.*

"Have fun. Nice to meet you Jamie," I call out, remembering we still need to discuss that. I turn to Drew after they disappear. "Where do you want to eat?"

"My place. You are on the menu." He grabs me in a hug and lifts me off my feet. I giggle, and even though I know others notice, I don't care.

"I thought you told Troy we were going out to eat," I say. Drew takes my hand and leads me back toward his truck on the other side of the bleachers.

"Would you rather I tell a white lie or tell him what I really want to do to his mother?"

"Good call," I laugh.

"I think there are some secrets we can keep from him."

"Yes. Smart," I say.

"I am!" he says as we pass the dugout, and I notice the floodlights are out, and the parking lot is bathed in dim light from the street. He scoops me up and throws me over his shoulder.

"What are you doing?" I say.

"I'm practicing my skills." I laugh as he jogs toward the truck. Opening the door, he plops me down like

I weigh nothing. "Time to get you home and practice some other skills."

I squeal, trying to remember how old I am because, damn, I feel like a teenage girl right now. *How does he do this to me?*

26

CONFESSIONS

CHARLEY

I'm full of paint as I wipe my finger again to type out a message to Drew.

> I got the ceiling done.

I send a selfie of my paint splattered face. Who would have thought home do-it-yourself could be so messy yet so satisfying? Even with the house feeling upside down, the vision of what my future will be is clear.

I open the can of trim paint and grab a clean brush. Might as well keep going. My phone dings, and I glance at the message.

> Aren't you the cutest painter I've ever seen?

> Thanks, I won't quit my day job lol

> Ha! Can't wait to see the daily results. I'm heading to do an inspection. Keep sending me updates. I hope you have our playlist on.

> I will. I do.

I send another picture of the Bluetooth speaker.

Love it!

:)

I put my phone aside and turn up the volume on my speaker as the lyrics fill the room. "Never get enough. It's a better life, so baby trust. Don't you wanna know? What it feels like…" I belt out the chorus, knowing only Miss Camilla can hear me, and she doesn't seem to mind when I sing a little off-key.

Drew and I have a shared playlist to collect songs we enjoy. It was his idea to keep me company when he's away at the station.

When he added, "Where's my love?" last week, I cried. He didn't know it would have that effect on me, and he apologized.

"Don't you dare apologize!" I said. I knew he had a little romantic inside him all this time. I promised not to give away his secret. As I start on the window trim, I stop singing and let my thoughts wander to the conversation we had last night on the phone.

***

"Oh, it's so nice to hear your voice. How much time do we have?" I ask.

"All the time in the world, unless you hear the alarm, of course," he reminds me. *That is the deal.* Alarm means a quick hang-up and a promise that he will contact me when he can. I am glad we have the in-between times to connect. He is much better at that now.

"Perfect. I've been thinking about some stuff, and since it's on my mind... " I say.

"Tell me what's on your mind, my girl. I can tell from your tone it won't wait," he says.

"I want to talk about bondage. You know, tie me up and have your way with me?"

"Is Troy home? I hope he can't hear you," he says, concerned.

"No, he's out with Jamie. He's so distracted with her now I think I could have a party beside him, and he wouldn't notice." I laugh.

"And as long as there is food in the fridge," he adds. "Is he doing okay now that he has started his senior year?"

"Yes, I am a little concerned about the biology course he's taking. I thought he would do more business courses, but I guess Jamie is in bio, so he added it." I shake my head, knowing his motivations. Apparently, they are lab partners. "We can talk about this later. You are here for supper on Thursday? You can get all the details then."

"Yes, that is the plan. Sounds like you want me to get details because he won't tell you everything?" The tone in his voice changes slightly, and I know he's teasing. We both agree that Troy seems to tell Drew stuff that I just can't pull out of him, no matter how I ask the question.

"Yes, fine. You see my motivation. Now stop changing the subject," I giggle.

"Yes, my girl," he growls low, and it amplifies in my ear. "You enjoyed it when I tied your hands together last time?" I respond instantly to the memory, and the low growl sends a flush to my cheeks.

"Very much," I answer with an exhale. *How did he switch my thoughts so quickly?*

"Do you have a request?" he says.

I pause, sorting through all the requests piled in my mind—remembering which one I wanted to discuss tonight. "Yes, I have a few options for us to consider."

"Options?" he asks.

"Yes, I did some shopping." My choices are all saved in my cart. I'm hopeful he will say yes to one of them.

"Oh my, you have piqued my interest. Show me." I glance around the house and open my laptop to the website. It's just me and Miss Camilla, no sign of Troy. *Don't be paranoid; you will hear him come home.*

The images fill my screen. I can see the details and descriptions so much better than on my phone. "I have the options ready," I say.

"Okay, I want you to narrow it down to three. Send me one at a time and tell me why you like them." His tone is very direct, and I enjoy having the parameters, but how do I narrow my cart of eight items down to three?

"Okay, give me a moment." I put him on speaker so I can type and scroll. I scan, realizing some are similar, so I click the 'remove' button and keep four options. I'll figure out between the last two later. "Okay, sending a pic of the first one."

I take a picture of my laptop screen. It's a little grainy, but he will get the idea. It's a set of metal cuffs covered in pink fabric. "I like the colour, and they look soft," I say as I hear him report he received the image.

"Got it. They look like something I've seen in a movie," he says.

"Oh! What movies are you watching?" I tease.

"I'll show you later. I don't think that is the best option. I don't like the metal, and we might lose the key."

"Good point! Next?" I say. I send the next image, which is a set of four Velcro cuffs with a hogtie attachment. It might be a little more than he was expecting, but when I saw it, my imagination ran wild with possibilities.

"Well, that's something I didn't expect," he says. I wish I could see his face. "Tell me why you like that?" he asks.

"Well, we could use two or all four," I say, hesitating, but what is the point? *I confess the desire, why be shy about it?*

"That little attachment connects all four cuffs together behind my back, making it almost impossible to move. Think about all the ways you could touch me," I add.

"Can I test your pleasure/pain tolerance with that option?" he asks.

My inner dirty girl can barely contain her excitement. I moan.

"I'll take that as a yes."

Damn it, didn't take long for him to flip that switch again.

"I wish you were here to see how much I like that image." I am so turned on by these ideas I bite my lip to control myself.

"You do not know how much you are turning me on right now. God damn."

Before I can get too distracted, I send him the next item from my cart. I'm going out on a limb a little, unsure what he will say. *I want to know his reaction.*

"Got it. Oh my, you keep surprising me. A spreader bar?" he asks.

"Yes, with cuffs. The bar extends too," I tell him as I take him off speaker so I can hear him better.

"I would love to see your legs spread like that," he says. There is a pause. I'm not sure what he will say next, but I want to rub my thighs together to create some friction. *I need a release.*

"I decided. It's number two. I want the hogtie attachment. I can't wait to see how it will look on you." he says, the growl in my ear turning me on. *That smooth, sexy voice.*

"Sold," I say. "Give me a minute to check out." I click the purchase box and enter my payment method.

"Take your time. Make sure you don't buy more than that. I know you are tempted," he says, and I laugh. *He's right.* I review the details before clicking *process.* My phone dings with a notification, but I don't look.

"All done. It says it will be here in three days."

"Wow, that is fast. Check your email, please," he says. I check my phone and see he has transferred me the cash to pay for the new cuffs. "You didn't have to do that," I say.

"Yes, I did. They are my cuffs now. I own them, which means I will use them whenever I want on MY girl. Got it?" he says.

I think I need to check my panties. "Got it. Thank you," I answer.

"What are you doing now?" he asks. I might have to go use my rabbit to help relieve some of the throbbing between my legs. *Do I tell him that?*

"I was thinking I would head to bed soon," I say, unsure if he will know what I mean.

"I have a request for you," he says.

"Oh?"

"Yes, I want you to settle in bed and start imagining all the ways I'm going to use my new cuffs on you. Then tomorrow, I want a complete confession," he says.

Oh, my good gawd! How did I find this man who knows exactly what I need?

"Yes, sir," I say.

"Good girl." He breathes out in another semi-growl, and I answer with a breathy sigh. "Night, Charley, can't wait to hear all about what else you have in that imagination of yours."

"Night." I hang up and close my laptop. *Did that just happen?*

***

My thoughts snap back to reality, and I notice "One of Them Girls" playing in the background. I've got the first coat of the trim done in my trancelike state and realize it's not such a bad way to spend a day off. Imagining ways of being pleasured and creating my new home.

"Life is good," I say to Miss Camilla, but as I turn, she is nowhere in sight.

"Talking to yourself again, Mom?" Troy's voice startles me as I turn to face him.

"AHH! Don't sneak up on me like that!" I say, realizing the paintbrush I was holding is now across the room.

"Sorry. I'm grabbing some stuff, heading out again," he says to the hallway.

"Heading out where?" Is it so difficult to give me answers to my face? I hear muffled answers, but I can't hear the words, so I follow Troy into his room.

"Mom, I love you, but you can't just come in here like that."

"Pardon?" Is he giving me attitude right now? Nothing that gets me more upset than a 'but' after 'I love you'. I see him shove something from his nightstand into his bookbag. *What is he doing?*

"Never mind, I'm heading out to see Jamie," he says, grabbing a jacket off the chair near his desk.

"Will you be home for supper?" I ask, moving to the side, trying not to block the door so he feels attacked.

"No, she said I can eat at her house. Her parents said yes," he adds, and I cock an eyebrow.

"Maybe Jamie should come here on Thursday for supper?" I ask. If this is getting more serious, I should try to get to know her. *Oh shit, Drew will be here too.* I almost kick myself for saying that day since I was hoping Drew would get details from him about Jamie. I guess that changes things.

"Drew is done with his rotation, and I wanted to have a nice meal here."

Troy moves things around on his desk, putting random objects in his bag.

I don't ask why. Maybe he's just trying not to make eye contact.

"I'm making fajitas... your favourite," I add in a singsong voice.

"Sure, I'll ask her. Can I go now?" he says.

"Sure." I move into the hallway, and he gives me a quick hug before rushing past me.

"Make good choices!" I call out as the door slams. *God knows I didn't at my age.* Moody teenage boys, how else do I deal? I pick up my phone.

> **Change of plans for Thursday. I invited Jamie to join us for supper.**

> **Hope that is okay.**

I wait for the bubbles to appear. Nothing. I'm sure he won't mind. Drew seems to be okay with the wild ride of raising a teenager. *Wait. Is that what is next?* Maybe I should talk to him about it. Is that what he wants?

Way to overthink the situation! Now I've ruined the buzzing pleasure of letting my imagination go wild at being hogtied to co-parenting with my new boyfriend. *Damn it.*

Direct and open communication, that's the rule. *Put this on the shelf for now and talk to him when he's not at the station.* This is a face-to-face convo.

I sigh and get back to putting the paint supplies away. Time to get cleaned up. I glance at my phone one more time. Nothing.

I want to text him my thoughts but hover over the letters. *Don't do it.*

The bubbles appear... he's responding.

I re-read the message a few times. My breath quickens, and the tears fall. *Damn it.* He doesn't even know what I'm thinking! Am I reading too much into this? Another text comes quickly, and I have to wipe my eyes to read it properly.

He's reading my mind. *How does he do that?*

I do.

I put my phone down and let the tears fall. Sobs wreak my body before I can process why I'm having such a strong reaction. I don't understand it, but it doesn't matter. Let it out. Let go.

I'm not alone anymore. I'm not alone.

EPILOGUE

DREW

I left work early so I could see Gran before heading to Charley's for supper. Aunt Christine texted me, calling her *your grandmother*, which clearly tells me she is pissed. As I open the door, I knock twice. "Hello?"

"NO, Mom!" I hear from the back room.

"Hello?" I call out again and move toward the voices.

"You can't go now." Aunt Christine says as she picks clothing out of a suitcase and moves it back onto the bed.

I knock on the bedroom door to announce my arrival. "See, Andrew is here now; he will tell you what I'm telling you."

I glare at her with a *do not put me in the middle of your argument* look.

"He will take me," Gran announces and puts her hands over her chest in a defiant stance.

"Hi, Gran," I say, ignoring their comments and approaching Gran to kiss her on the cheek. I notice she seems to have her strength back, and her color looks great. Did she do her hair?

"I'm not sure what this is all about. Fill me in." I sit in the chair by the window, noticing the view of the neighbour's fence. I've not sat down to truly take in the new room that Aunt Christine made for her. She claimed it was 'lovely', but what is so lovely about a twelve-by-twelve room with white walls and only the basic furniture? The institution-like feel of the room makes my skin crawl.

"I want to go to the lake house. Can you drive me?" Gran says, sitting on her single bed on top of the clothes piled there.

"Not today," Aunt Christine chimes in as she folds clothes.

"I agree with Aunt Christine. I can't today. I just got home. How about I take you next weekend? We can check on the place and maybe take a few more of the boxes that are in storage," I say. My negotiation doesn't seem to influence her, and her expression hardens. I see the lines between her eyes get deeper.

"If I have to stay one more day with that excuse of a man, my daughter calls a husband..." Gran says.

"Mom! He can hear you," Aunt Christine cuts her off.

"Oh, is that the issue?" I ask.

"Of course, that is the issue. The control freak won't let me do anything around here." She shouts, and I know it's on purpose because of the way she spits out her words toward my aunt.

"He was just worried about you going for a walk by yourself," Aunt Christine explains.

I can see she is trying very hard to control her anger, knowing it will make things worse with my grandmother.

"Well, I want to leave," Gran announces and then looks at me. "I want you to take me today. I'll be fine there by myself."

Stubborn woman. I admire her for it, but right now, this is a pain in the ass.

"Why do you want to go when the lake house isn't ready? We agreed you would move there this spring?" I say, trying to help her see reason.

"Because I can't spend all winter here with that man. I'll wither and die," she says as she gets the pile of clothes Aunt Christine just folded and drops them into her suitcase. *Now, we have resorted to the dramatic.* Great.

"Gran, I can't take you today, but I can take you tomorrow," I say.

Aunt Christine glares at me.

"But," I say, knowing that this needs to be resolved so cooler heads prevail. "Aunt Christine is invited to come with us. We will look at the lake house and make a plan. You are not moving there yet until I know it's set up properly."

They both look at me, weighing my words.

"Understand?" I ask, but it's not a question. I think this is the only way to deal with this from here on in. I'm putting my foot down.

"Aunt Christine will put your things away. Grab your purse, you are coming with me," I say to Gran.

I turn to my aunt and say, "I want to visit with her for a bit. I'll bring her back by eight o'clock."

She nods in gratitude, and I see her shoulders slump. The weight of looking after her mother must feel so heavy. *I should help more.*

I move toward Aunt Christine with open arms, realizing that I don't hug her very often. She lets me envelop her, and I whisper, "Sorry, I'll be here more often to help. I'm here now."

Part of me is glad I can take some of the burden from her, and the other part is concerned about how I can make good on my promise.

I hear a quiet 'thank you' in my chest, and I let her go. She turns away to fold the clothes again, and I see her wipe her eyes.

"Come on, Gran, let's go get some fajitas."

I help Gran get into my truck and pull out my phone to text Charley. I hope she won't mind. *Of course, she won't.*

> **Change of plans. Gran is with me. I'll explain later.**

> **You okay if I bring her for supper?**

I watch for the bubbles, and they appear. Disappear. Appear. Disappear. Appear. I look at the sky. "Margaret, please help me with this."

Oh, thank god.

> **ME: Of course. Text me the list, and I'll get dessert, too.**

> **Thank you! Troy is here waiting for Jamie to show up. He's driving me crazy, so don't be too long.**

> **I'll be there in thirty minutes.**

> **Can't wait to see you. I've missed you, but you know that already.**

> **What I'm going to do to you later will make up for our missed time.**

> **See you soon.**

I hop into the truck without waiting for her reply and start the engine. "All buckled in?"

"Where are we going?" Gran asks.

"We are going to see my new girlfriend, Gran. I think you will like her," I say, smiling.

"My Drew has a girlfriend?" she says, clapping her hands together.

"Yes," I laugh. "But first, we need to stop and get some of your favourite cupcakes. We don't want to show up empty-handed," I say.

The smile that splits her face showing her excitement, makes my insides melt.

"I think that is the best news all day," she says.

"Me too," I sigh and hope maybe for a moment she will forget about moving to the lake house and I don't have to commit to renovations this fall. I have so many other things I want to do first. Mainly spending every moment I can with Charley.

"What is her name? Do I know her? Is it Jennifer?" Gran rapid fires questions, and I can feel her curiosity building. *Jennifer? Do I know a Jennifer?*

"It's Charley Thomas, you know her. She works at the bookstore," I say.

"Charley?" she asks. I try to gauge her enthusiasm. "She has a child, Drew. A teenager." That wasn't a question. That was a warning.

"Yes, Gran. I'm aware of her son, Troy. He's a great kid. You will get to meet him tonight," I say.

"Oh, that will be nice," she says, though there's a slight hesitation in her voice. I feel the weight of unspoken words between us, but I don't ask her thoughts; I know my own mind, and they won't change my decision.

"I'm with Charley now. I know you're happy for me, Gran," I say, taking her hand and giving it a gentle squeeze.

She looks at me, her eyes softening. "Of course, dear," she says, and this time her voice is steady. She presses my hand, a silent promise in her touch. "You've grown up strong, Drew. And Charley... she's lucky to have you."

The knot in my chest loosens, and a quiet relief settles over me. "Thank you, Gran," I whisper, leaning in to kiss her cheek. The moment is small, but it feels like a blessing, grounding me in everything that's to come.

ACKNOWLEDGEMENTS

Writing a book is never a solo journey, and this one is no exception. My heartfelt thanks go out to everyone who has been by my side along the way.

To my early readers and trusted confidantes—your feedback gave this book its rhythm, its heartbeat, and its bite. A special thanks to Kenzie and Alison. Having you both eager to know Charley's world kept me going, especially on the days when I wasn't sure I could find the brainpower to write.

To my incredible team: my editor, Caroline Goldsworthy, thank you for your sharp eye and insightful feedback—you've helped shape this book into something I'm truly proud of. To the artistic team who created the cover, your stunning artwork has brought this story to life in a way I couldn't have imagined. And to my book coach, Joe Gilbert, thank you for your guidance and encouragement throughout this entire process. I now know the power of tracking in an Excel spreadsheet and am not ashamed to claim my obsessive side!

To my fellow romance writers, who were willing to let me ask a million questions and encouraged me every step of the way—you made the long writing days feel not so lonely.

To my family—thank you for your endless love, patience, and support. You've given me the time and encouragement to pursue my passion, and I couldn't have done this without you.

To James, for always insisting on being my alpha reader and never failing to tell me how amazed you were with my storytelling, even when it wasn't. Thank you for being willing to learn what was in my head and encouraging me to write every day. My persistence and discipline on the hard days were all to make you proud.

And to you, dear reader—thank you for choosing this story, for stepping into the mess and magic of

Mountmooke Bay. If it made you laugh, cry, or feel even a little less alone, then I've done what I came here to do.

With all my love and gratitude,

Elizabeth

xoxo

www.ingramcontent.com/pod-product-compliance
Lightning Source LLC
Chambersburg PA
CBHW070314310726

48976CB00005B/1706